ALLEN COUNTY PUBLIC LIBRARY

P9-BHR-336

Confessions of a bad girl wannabe?

Well, not exactly. I never actually wanted to be one of *those* girls. At least, not the sleazy, too-tight-Lycra, jump-anything-that-moves kind of girl.

But I did want…something.

And I wasn't getting it by being the girl next door, that's for sure. I mean, when this all started, I was twenty-seven years old and I'd never even worn thong underwear. I'd never had cybersex. And I certainly hadn't ever done *it* anyplace even remotely public.

I guess, when you get right down to it, I just wanted sex. Good sex. Amazingly Good Sex. With a capital *A,* and a capital *G* and a capital *S.* And frankly, I wasn't getting any.

Which meant I was on a mission to remedy that little problem…

AUG 0 2 2006

Blaze™

Dear Reader,

This book has had a long and bumpy path. I originally wrote the proposal right before chick lit really hit the market in a huge way. In its original incarnation, the book was not a romance, and poor Mike (the hero) wasn't even a figment of my imagination. My agent shopped the proposal, and we received tons of wonderful feedback about the clever premise and my voice. What we didn't receive, however, was an offer.

Fast forward a few years, and suddenly I *am* writing chick lit. (I'm writing a trilogy of chick-lit thrillers for Downtown Press and a series of paranormal mommy-lit books for Berkley.) But *The Perfect Score* didn't fit with the type of chick lit I was publishing. No demons. No codes or assassins. What to do, what to do?

Enter Brenda Chin, my editor at Harlequin. When I complained that the only thing on my mind at the moment was this old chick-lit proposal that I wanted very much to bring back to life, she announced that Harlequin Blaze was now offering chick lit. So, yes, I should send her some pages, because this sounded like a perfect fit. Yay!

This was probably the longest "labor" of all of my books, but I think it was worth it. Hopefully you will, too!

(And just as an interesting tidbit, if you're interested in knowing which scenes were in the original proposal submitted all those years ago, visit www.juliekenner.com and find the dedicated page for *The Perfect Score*.)

Happy reading,

Julie Kenner

JULIE KENNER
The Perfect Score

HARLEQUIN®

TORONTO • NEW YORK • LONDON
AMSTERDAM • PARIS • SYDNEY • HAMBURG
STOCKHOLM • ATHENS • TOKYO • MILAN • MADRID
PRAGUE • WARSAW • BUDAPEST • AUCKLAND

If you purchased this book without a cover you should be aware that this book is stolen property. It was reported as "unsold and destroyed" to the publisher, and neither the author nor the publisher has received any payment for this "stripped book."

ISBN-13: 978-0-373-79273-3
ISBN-10:   0-373-79273-5

THE PERFECT SCORE

Copyright © 2006 by Julia Beck Kenner.

All rights reserved. Except for use in any review, the reproduction or utilization of this work in whole or in part in any form by any electronic, mechanical or other means, now known or hereafter invented, including xerography, photocopying and recording, or in any information storage or retrieval system, is forbidden without the written permission of the publisher, Harlequin Enterprises Limited, 225 Duncan Mill Road, Don Mills, Ontario, Canada M3B 3K9.

All characters in this book have no existence outside the imagination of the author and have no relation whatsoever to anyone bearing the same name or names. They are not even distantly inspired by any individual known or unknown to the author, and all incidents are pure invention.

This edition published by arrangement with Harlequin Books S.A.

® and TM are trademarks of the publisher. Trademarks indicated with ® are registered in the United States Patent and Trademark Office, the Canadian Trade Marks Office and in other countries.

www.eHarlequin.com

Printed in U.S.A.

ABOUT THE AUTHOR

National bestselling author Julie Kenner spent four years mainlining venti nonfat lattes in order to write, practice law full-time and take care of her kiddo. Then she wised up, quit the practice of law and settled down to write full-time. Her books have won numerous awards and hit bestseller lists as varied as *USA TODAY*, *Locus* magazine, Waldenbooks and Barnes & Noble. Visit Julie on the Web at www.juliekenner.com.

Books by Julie Kenner

HARLEQUIN BLAZE

HARLEQUIN TEMPTATION

Don't miss any of our special offers. Write to us at the following address for information on our newest releases.

Harlequin Reader Service
U.S.: 3010 Walden Ave., P.O. Box 1325, Buffalo, NY 14269
Canadian: P.O. Box 609, Fort Erie, Ont. L2A 5X3

For Brenda, who gave this book a home.
And to the Temptresses, particularly whoever mentioned,
all those years ago, the Internet Slut Test that
sparked the idea for this book!

1

"EIGHTEEN PERCENT!" I could hear my voice echoing through the cinderblock-walled laundry room. "Eighteen percent is for nuns and small children. Eighteen percent is not for twenty-seven-year-old single girls living in Los Angeles."

Carla yanked open the dryer and started scooping her pinkish whites into her laundry basket. An hour ago, her whites had actually been white, but with Carla, these things tended to happen. "I still can't believe you're so upset just because you got a crappy score on some Internet Slut Test." She flashed me a look designed to underscore just how much she didn't believe I'd do something so foolish. Ridiculous, really, given that Carla had known me since kindergarten. I was Mattie Brown and she was Carla Browning, which meant that fate had pretty much destined that we'd sit beside each other in every class until graduation. Being relatively pragmatic, we figured we could either be best friends or vile enemies. We'd opted for the friend route. At the time, it had seemed the more prudent option.

Today, Carla was probably having second thoughts, a supposition that quickly proved true when she pulled out a pale pink bra and shook it at me. "You're as bad as you were in high school, only now you don't have Angie dogging your heels."

Angie is my stepsister, although the "step" part has never really been part of the equation for either one of us. We were both three when our parents married, and she's my sister, for good, bad or indifferent. And since we're separated by a mere four months (she's the eldest), we grew up sharing each other's clothes, coveting each other's boyfriends and busting tail to outdo each other academically, socially and every other way. I love her, but I've never stopped trying to beat her. And—damn the woman—the truth is that she usually beat me. In everything from boyfriends to grade point average. (In the latter, she edged by me with one grade point, taking the lead in our very last semester of high school, and wresting the valedictorian slot away from me. Not that I'm bitter or anything…)

I took a breath and tried to stop scowling. "I'm not trying to be the slut valedictorian. For that matter, it's not even really about the test. I mean, another test said my perfect job would be analyzing actuarial tables, and how *ewww* is that?"

"Very," she agreed, and we both paused for a moment, reveling in the mathematical horror. "But if it wasn't the test, then what?"

I shrugged. "The realization that came with it, I guess." I paused for emphasis, then spit out the horrible truth. "My sex life is boring."

Carla's perfectly plucked brows rose infinitesimally. "I thought you didn't have a sex life?"

So much for slipping one past Carla. "Fine. You win. My sex life *was* boring. Back when I was with Dex, it was duller than dirt. And now that I'm single again, it's not boring. It's nonexistent." Dex had dumped me about four months ago, a little fact that had pretty much blown me out of the water. We'd been together two years, and I expected we'd stay together, ending up with a marriage and two-point-five kids and a dog.

Yes, our sex life—and the rest of our relationship if you want to get right down to it—had been spiraling downward, but we were *comfortable*. Or, at least I'd thought we were.

But my dirty little secret? Even though I was blindsided by the breakup, I wasn't all that disappointed. What I was, was angry. I should have been the dumper, not the dumpee. As it was, I'd completely lost face. With myself, even if with no one else.

With a dramatic sigh, I hefted an armful of white cotton undies out of my dryer, then frowned at the laundry basket, wishing it were filled with shocking bits of red satin and black lace. Underwear with a raison d'être more provocative than simply keeping my private parts hidden in the event of a catastrophic highway accident. Like every other normal mother on the planet, my high-powered attorney mom's list of constant worries placed clean underwear higher than poverty, nuclear war or starving children in China.

Too bad for me, Mom had taught me well. There wasn't a frivolous panty in the bunch. No satin, no lace, nothing even remotely Frederick's of Hollywood about my unmentionables. Not even Victoria's Secret. We're talking K-Mart all the way.

No wonder I wasn't a slut.

I sighed dramatically and leaned against the detergent dispenser. "My sex life is boring. My clothes are boring. My life is boring."

Carla frowned at another light pink shirt, then waved the hideous thing in my direction. "Want a pink tee?"

What I wanted was to strangle her. Here I was having a relatively dramatic personal crisis and she was ruining her laundry. "Have you even heard a word I've said?"

3 1833 05030 3749

This time, she really did give me her attention, and frankly, considering her scowl, I wasn't certain I wanted it. "Look, Mattie—"

"I mean it. I'm going to do it. By this time next year, I'm blowing the roof off that stupid test."

This time, she raised only a single eyebrow, a trick I envied mightily.

"I'm serious. That's my New Year's resolution."

"There's an entire universe of possibilities out there, and you're wasting a perfectly good resolution on acing a sex test?"

"You want to say that a little louder? I'm not sure they heard you by the pool." I poked my head out the open laundry-room door, scanning for eavesdroppers. Katy Simmons, the retired actress who lived below me, was sunning on a lounge chair. The new tenant—Mike Something-or-other—was a bit closer. A genuinely nice guy, he was also the apartment complex's resident nerd, complete with wire-framed glasses and a job that had something to do with computers.

As I watched, I could see him settle himself in one of the incredibly uncomfortable metal chairs, kick his feet up onto a tabletop, and take a swig of beer. I took a breath, surprised that my nerdish neighbor had a mighty fine body, lean and firm like a swimmer.

"Mike!" Carla half yelled. "Oh, Mikey! Mattie needs a boyfriend!"

"Carla!" I grabbed the knob and slammed the door shut. "Are you insane? What if he heard?"

"So what if he did? He's cute."

I scowled, because he *was* cute. He was nice, too. I'd helped him carry boxes up from his U-Haul, and he'd happily shared his pizza with me a week ago. But Dex had been cute and nice, too. Cute and nice didn't cut it anymore. Cute and nice conjured the dreaded *R* word, and I wasn't anywhere near ready to get back on that relationship hamster wheel. "I'm not looking for cute. Cute is for bunny rabbits. Not boy toys."

Another lift of that eyebrow of hers.

I sighed and tried to look put-upon. "You just don't understand. You're getting laid on a regular basis."

"So were you until you dumped Dex."

I shook my head vehemently, my ponytail whipping around to slap me in the face. "Oh, no, no, no my friend. I was only having sorta-sex."

She flashed me a skeptical look as she shook the wrinkles out of a pair of greyish-pink sweatpants. "I'm going to regret asking, but what is sorta-sex?"

"You know. Fridays only. Me on my back. After *Law & Order,* but before *Biography.* Routine all the way. Nothing spontaneous. Nothing romantic. I could put Tollhouse cookies in before we went at it and not have to worry that they'd burn."

"Oh. Well." She busied herself with neatly folding her now-ruined laundry, while I silently cheered myself for having a sex life so truly pathetic that I'd rendered Carla speechless. Scary, I know, but I take my victories where I find them.

"Well," she said again, and I felt my victory slipping away. True, I wanted her help. I just couldn't handle her pity. "That's not so bad," she finally said, in a you're-bankrupt-and-your-dog-died-but-it'll-be-okay kind of voice. "I mean, it was still sex, right?"

This from the woman whose boyfriend just might be a superhero named Erection-Man. Mitch would come over after work, see her puttering in her kitchen wearing a ratty T-shirt and gym socks, and get so turned-on he'd bend her over the table and have his way with her. "We live in different universes, Carla," I said.

To her credit, she looked a little sheepish. It wasn't as though she didn't realize how fabulous her sex life was. But then, Carla's one of those beautiful people. Perfect face, perfect hair, perfect skin, perfect job. No lumps, no bumps, not even a tiny acne scar. Smart, too. The kind of woman you'd want to kill if she weren't so darn *nice.*

"Have you put any thought into when you're going to do the legwork necessary to reach this nirvana of sexual prowess?"

I made a face. Mostly because Carla was being typically Carla and reverting to what I call her adult-speak voice—which is what she does whenever she thinks anyone is acting like an idiot. But also because, frankly, I *hadn't* put any thought into my newly announced resolution.

"That's what I thought," Carla said, making me scowl even more. "I mean, come on, Mattie. You've been working like a fiend for months. This is your first weekend off in forever."

That was true enough. I work at John Layman Productions, and if the company sounds familiar, then you're probably one of those people who watches really bad reality programming about celeb-rities that no one cares about anymore. Not that I'm criticizing my boss's chosen field or anything (ahem). I mean, it pays the bills. But, honestly, does anyone *really* care about kids who were celebrities when they were six, then fell off the map during the last two decades? And if somebody *does* care enough to tune in every night at eleven, then, you know, maybe that person just needs to get a life.

All JLP programs have excellent ratings, though.

So either I'm wrong, or there are a whole lot of people out there with no life whatsoever.

In fact, there are so many people out there tuning in that JLP is adding five new shows to our already overstuffed production schedule. And that, as Carla pointed out, is keeping me tethered to the office and, late in the evening, to my home computer. In fact, the only reason I have this weekend off is because the company's computer network crashed. Since John's currently following some stick-thin, party girl celebrity around Rio, he actually shut work down for a long weekend while the computer gurus do their thing. Amazing, but true. (Although he did instruct our furniture supplier to deliver a bookshelf and lateral filing cabinet to my apartment so that I can, in the words of my boss, "work even more efficiently on evenings and weekends." Yeah, love you too, John. At the moment, four very large, very heavy boxes are sitting in my living room, waiting for me to suck it up and begin assembling my home office suite.

Carla also works in television. Her boss, however, is Timothy Pierpont, the Emmy- and Oscar-winning producer who's giving Bruckheimer and Bochco a run for their money with his original, provocative programming. What did I tell you? Carla, perfect. Me, perfectly wretched.

As I pondered my wretchedness, I noticed that Carla was tapping her chin with her index finger, a sure sign that she was deep in thought.

"What?" I demanded.

"I'm just thinking that maybe your schedule *can* work to your benefit," she said.

"Explain, please."

"If you have no free time, then no one will get the impression it's about commitment. It must be a fling, because who has time for anything else?"

"Right," I said, drawing out the word as I tried to anticipate where she was going.

Carla, however, sped up, her voice channeling my earlier enthusiasm. "You should go for it. Definitely. Get out there and have a wild time." She leaned back, her arms crossed over her chest and a smug smile brightening her face. "And I know just how you should start."

I narrowed my eyes, smelling a trick. "How?"

"Cullen Slater." She spoke the name like an incantation, then waited for me to react. She didn't have long to wait.

"Have you gone mental?" Dark and dangerous, Slater was a very gainfully employed male model who alternated between a Ferrari and a Harley, sported a perfect five o'clock shadow no matter the time of day, and tended to date women whose clothes consisted of colorful adhesive strips. Well, *date* may give the wrong impression since I never saw any of his women more than once. But our apartments shared a common wall, and I can say with absolute certainty that none of his women left Slater's apartment unsatisfied. Or well rested.

Cullen Slater is the reason I started sleeping with earplugs. Considering my newly announced resolution, I should probably trash the earplugs and buy a vibrator.

Carla's coral-pink lips curved in smug satisfaction. "You've seen the kind of girls he's always dragging up the stairs at three in the morning."

"Slater is a god among men," I said. "And I *have* seen those women. There's no way he'd be interested in me."

Carla lifted one shoulder in a dainty gesture. "Don't sell yourself short, Mat. He's gorgeous, yes, but you're not too shabby. And you're brilliant and articulate and what guy wouldn't want you?"

I let that one hang, because in my experience with guys like Cullen—as in, guys whose talents run more toward the camera than the cognitive—*brilliant* and *articulate* weren't that much of an asset. Come to think of it, those two traits weren't exactly a selling point to *any* man, IQ notwithstanding. Breasts, I think, were the common denominator among men. And on that score, I was definitely only average.

Carla, however, was on a roll. "And he always asks you to bring in his mail when he's out of town," she pointed out, "so we already know that he trusts you. He must like you, too. And if you can get Slater in your bed, you'll know you've reached some sort of slut nirvana."

My stomach did one of those dropping-off-a-cliff numbers.

Slater.

I took a deep breath, felt beads of sweat form on my forehead, and silently agreed that Cullen Slater was an idea worth pondering. Not to mention a goal worth reaching.

Cullen Slater. The consummate bad boy.

Slater. And me. Me and Slater.

In bed.

In me.

Oh my.

MIKE PETERSON COULDN'T concentrate on his book, even though he usually glommed on to anything and everything by Stephen King. Today, even a reread of the horrors that plagued poor Derry, Maine, couldn't compare to what he'd just heard as he'd been walking past the laundry room toward the pool.

Mattie Brown was looking to ratchet up her sex life.

He gripped the book a little bit tighter as an image of Mattie slipped into his mind. Her quick smile. The friendly waves as they passed on the stairs. The way she tossed her hair when she scanned her mail.

Get a grip, man.

The truth was, he'd fallen hard for her the first day he'd met her. Fifteen days ago, actually, when she'd blown off grocery shopping to help him schlep boxes from the U-Haul up to his brand-new apartment. She'd been wearing ratty gray sweatpants and a T-shirt that boldly exclaimed that A Woman Needs A Man Like A Fish Needs A Bicycle. When he'd commented on it, she'd blushed and explained that she'd bought the T-shirt a few months before, after a breakup with her longtime boyfriend.

He could still remember the little surge of relief— both that she was unattached and that the shirt didn't necessarily reflect her overall opinion of the male of the species.

Ever since that first encounter, he'd been intending to ask her out. Coffee at one of the little shops down on Ventura Boulevard. Maybe a movie. Even pizza by the pool. But damned if work hadn't kept him booked solid for the past two weeks. Not that he could complain. Getting the *Menagerie* gig had been a huge coup, and he was more than willing to work his tail off for as long as MonkeyShines, Inc. was willing to pay him.

He'd worked in the computer gaming industry for years, but this was the first time he'd headed up a project since he'd gone freelance eighteen months ago. The fact that he'd scored the job at the same time he'd moved from Austin to Los Angeles had made life a little more hectic, but it had also satisfied that niggling fear that he wouldn't be able to pay the bills.

Bottom line: the job came first. Women—even women as tempting as Mattie, whose scent alone had driven him nuts—were off-limits until the project was well under control.

He smiled a little to himself, wondering if Grandma Jo had been right—he really did have a guardian angel. Because how else could he explain the fortuitous convergence of events? Him finishing up Phase One of the *Menagerie* project right as Mattie was looking to add a little more spice to her life? And—more importantly—him being in the right place at the right time to hear about Mattie's New Year's resolution.

He took another swig of beer, casually wishing

that he could have heard the rest of their conversation. He'd heard the first part only by happenstance, since he'd come the back way to the pool, circling around the laundry room because he'd gone to the parking garage first to get the Stephen King novel from his car. Their voices hadn't been high so much as urgent. At least, Mattie's had.

As soon as he'd recognized her voice, he'd slowed his pace, hoping to find an opening where he could pop into the laundry room. Maybe say hi. Casually suggest a coffee sometime.

But as soon as he'd realized the topic of their discussion, he'd known that any interruption would not only embarrass the heck out of Mattie, it would also kill any chance he'd ever have of taking her out on a proper date.

What he should have done was leave. Right then. That instant. But his guardian angel had sprouted horns and a tail, and he'd hung around, then overheard the delicious, decadent New Year's resolution that Mattie had proposed.

Mike had been tempted to loiter and learn exactly what Mattie had in mind, but the devil on his shoulder had turned angelic again, and urged him to get out of there. Perfect timing, too, because not thirty seconds later, he heard Carla's high-pitched voice followed by Mattie's squeal and the appearance of her head around the door frame, as she scoped out the area, clearly looking for eavesdroppers.

He'd kept his eyes down, aimed at his book, and hoped that Mattie couldn't tell that he'd not only heard her state her goal, but that he was looking forward to helping her reach it.

Which, of course, raised the question of exactly how he was going to convince Mattie that he could provide invaluable assistance with her quest.

That, however, was the kind of academic problem he thrived on. He might have to flowchart it, script it, program it and then debug it…but somehow, someway, he was going to come up with the perfect plan. After all, he didn't have degrees from Stanford and MIT for nothing.

It was time to put his education to work. And he couldn't think of a single thing he'd rather score an A+ in than the seduction of Mattie Brown.

2

HERE IS MY PROBLEM with the do-it-yourself culture we now live in: We're expected to do all this stuff that professionals used to do, but no one has bothered to either a) train us, or b) give us the right freaking equipment.

Self-serve gas stations, for example. Okay, yes, sure. It's nice not to have to wait for—or chat with—Tommy Tune Up, but Tommy's absence from my life has caused me to burn oil on more than one occasion. I can fill up my car just fine, but those oil dipsticks are designed to be entirely unreadable by anyone lacking a Ph.D. in auto mechanics. It's true! It's like a nationwide conspiracy.

And furniture… Don't even get me started on furniture.

I have vivid memories of wonderful wooden pieces being delivered to my parents' house when I was a kid, hauled in on rolling dollies—fully assembled, mind you—by strapping young men working their way through college.

So why had those buff Adonises not delivered my furniture? I'll tell you why: Because some genius somewhere decided that they could draw a picture, include an Allen wrench and make me do it myself.

Honestly, it's enough to make a girl never want to have kids. Assemble toys on Christmas Eve? No thank you very much!

My future progeny notwithstanding, at the moment I had two shelves and a filing cabinet to assemble, and no Adonis to help with the project. Oh well. I'm a self-sufficient female, right? Absent any other options, I figured I could handle it myself.

I figured wrong.

An hour later, I'd manage to assemble only the bare frame of the first bookshelf, and that after having to remove and reinsert the first set of screws and little connector thingamabobs. Had the instructions been in English, perhaps I would have had better luck. Instead, the manufacturer had included only poorly drawn pictures of the various steps. And I'm ashamed to say I don't know how to translate hieroglyphics.

Frustrated, I tossed the Allen wrench, then made a rude sound when it skittered over the battered wood floor to rest under the couch. That, I figured, was a signal that it was time for a break. Or to call in reinforcements. Or both.

Buoyed by the thought of something cool and refreshing, I headed to the kitchen. I grabbed a Diet Coke from the fridge, popped the top, then took a sip before I called Carla. True, she'd just left an hour ago, but she only lived a stone's throw away. She'd gone home to put away her laundry and catch up on some housework before Mitch came back from his latest business outing. Considering the depths of Carla's hatred for toilet bowl scrubbing, I figured my odds of recruiting help were pretty darn high.

Again, unfortunately, I was wrong.

"I really wish I could give you a hand," she said, after I explained my dilemma. "But Mitch caught an earlier flight and he's already in a taxi."

"Oh," I said, knowing it was pointless to argue. Besides, I was happy for Carla. Happy and not the slightest bit envious. Nope. No green in my blood.

I cleared my throat. "Right. Well, guess I'll let you get back to it."

"You know, if John thinks it's so important that you have office furniture at home, maybe he should have hired someone to put it together for you."

"Yeah," I said, figuring that it would be more

likely that pink pigs would fly by my open window. "True enough."

Carla sighed, obviously understanding what I hadn't said: I'd never once defied my boss and I wasn't about to start now. "Listen, Mitch will probably go home early tomorrow. I mean, he's got to unpack, right? I could help you then."

"Great," I said, but without a lot of enthusiasm. I hung up the phone before she clued in to my suddenly miserable state. If Carla needed shelves assembled, she had Mitch. Me? I had neither a considerate boss nor a studly boy toy.

I leaned against the fridge and sighed, then took another sip of soda. The fact was, I was a neurotic mess. I mean, had I really announced to Carla that I wanted to up my score on a *slut test?* That was so *not* like me.

I called Carla back and told her that. She immediately laughed. "Are you kidding? That's exactly like you!"

"Excuse me?"

"In school, if you made a lousy grade, you obsessed about it until you got it right. That's why you're still working for ballbuster John, isn't it? Because you can't go somewhere else until you've made a huge success of that? Which is ridiculous, actually, because you never wanted to be the queen of reality television. But you're giving your life to the job. You haven't finished a new screenplay in months. It's your dream, Mattie, and you've stopped chasing it."

We'd had this particular conversation about a million times, with Carla pushing and me pushing right back. I'd taken the job to further my writing career, and Carla damn well knew that. Today, though, I wasn't in the mood to remind her. "This isn't about my job. It's about me. I mean, what normal person wants to up their Slut IQ?"

"Whoever said you're normal?" she countered. "And you're being ridiculous anyway. You and I both know it's not about being a slut."

"It's not?"

"Of course not," she said. "You just want to cut loose. Honestly, Mattie, it's about time. You said yourself that your sex life is boring. And it has been boring ever since your first date. Louis Dailey? I mean, come on! You could have done so much better."

I frowned at the phone. She had a point. I tended toward the safe guys. The nice guys. I wanted the spice in my life, but I think I was a little afraid that I was too…*something* for the bad boys. That they'd end up dumping me. And, yes, I was *waaaaay* too competitive to let that happen.

So I ended up with guys that *I* ultimately dumped. Guys without the adventurous quality that I craved. The wrong guys—I knew it from the start—but I hooked up anyway.

For years, I'd been living on the edge of a vicious—albeit comfortable—circle. Then Dex had gone and dumped *me* and my entire world view had shifted one-hundred-eighty degrees.

"A wild fling with Cullen is just the ticket," Carla said, apparently reading my mind. "He's definitely the guy to spice up a girl's sex life, but you know he's not boyfriend material, so it's not like you'd date him. So there's no emotional risk, you know?"

I did know. And it sounded delicious. In a superscary sort of way.

The truth is, I've always played life pretty safe. Studying my ass off in high school because I was terrified of a bad grade. A good college. An even better law school. Not because I wanted to be a lawyer but because my parents had pounded into my head that I needed a solid career. Hobbies—like my love of writing—were fine…so long as I didn't take them too seriously.

And so I'd emerged from school with a plan. Be an attorney. Get rich. Then do what I wanted. But I'd caught the Hollywood bug (to the chagrin of my mother who likes to pretend that Los Angeles is merely an economic center and not the heart of the film industry). I made the first unpredictable leap in my life—leaving law to take a television job.

I'd had night sweats for weeks before finally making the decision, but even then, I'd played it safe. I hadn't taken temp jobs to support my writing habit. No, I'd taken an executive-level job with a major production company for an extremely lucrative salary. I was secure, my mom was happy. And most important, I was safe.

Except that so far, safe hadn't paid off for me. Not in jobs (last I'd noticed, I had yet to win an Academy Award) and not in relationships. Looked at that way, I had to admit that scary might just be good for me.

And besides, Cullen Slater was a male model. A *male model*. As in über-hot. Odds were good he'd ignore me completely and I'd never be forced to face the sheer lunacy of my plan.

Thus reassured, I hung up from Carla once again, then stood there, peering into the living room. The bits of unassembled furniture were still scattered about. Apparently, the house fairies hadn't taken pity on me and assembled the things while I was taking my break.

I frowned at the couch, under which the Allen wrench still resided. I didn't want to rummage under there for the wrench any more than I wanted to sit on my rump staring at doodles that were supposed to be assembly instructions. This was my one rare weekend off! What the heck was John thinking, making me do construction work? Hadn't he ever heard of worker's comp? What if I hammered a finger? Or chipped my manicure?

I had a sudden mental image of John in khaki shorts and a Hawaiian shirt, panting after some former child star, hoping she'd either shoot up on camera or deign to sleep with him. And all the while, he'd be mainlining Bloody Marys and soaking up the sun.

With a picture like that in my head, is it any wonder I decided that Carla was right? Debauchery really was the way to go. And the damn furniture could wait. After all, I had relaxing of my own to do.

"MATTIE, RIGHT?"

The smooth, masculine voice wafted over me, and I peeled my eyes open, then looked up at him through my RayBans.

"Mike Peterson," he said, apparently in answer to my blank stare.

"Oh, right. I know. Hi." In my sunscreen and margarita-induced haze, I'd fantasized the voice belonged to Cullen, home early from this weekend's photo shoot. I hoped I didn't sound too disappointed.

He dragged a lounge chair closer. "Do you mind?"

"Um, no." That was a half lie. After abandoning furniture assembly, I'd rummaged in my cabinets until I found my blender, then repeated the process in the freezer until I found some limeade. The tequila didn't require a search. I keep it handy, right on top of the refrigerator. One can frozen concentrated LimeAid, a bunch of ice cubes, and a can full of tequila, and I was good to go.

I'd finished one glass and was nursing my second when Mike joined me. Since I'm a lightweight, I already had a nice little buzz going, and I was perfectly content to lie there in the sun, reveling in my newfound status as the rebel of John Layman Productions.

Still, I supposed I could manage to revel *and* be polite to the new guy. Especially a new guy who looked so damn sexy in swim trunks and a black Universal Studios Hollywood T-shirt. Too bad he was the computer geek, nice-guy type. Too much like Dex to be a candidate for my "guy to have a sexually adventurous relationship" plan. Besides, Carla and I had already picked Cullen. And he was, undoubtedly, perfect for the role.

"Playing tourist?" I asked, gazing meaningfully at the shirt.

He grinned, not at all embarrassed by the fashion

faux pas. (I mean, what L.A. local actually advertises the area attractions?) "I'm entitled," he said. "Until I stop confusing the Hollywood and Santa Monica freeways, I figure I am still a tourist."

The man had a point. "You'll get it down," I said. I pointed once again at the shirt. "So what was your favorite thing?"

"The *Back to the Future* ride," he said, referring to the amusement park ride where the guests climb into a mock-up of the famous DeLorean-turned-time-machine and then race around Hill Valley, narrowly avoiding all sorts of obstacles and, of course, barely escaping with their lives.

Since that's my favorite ride, too, (well, with the exception of the tram ride that takes you through the actual Universal back lot), I gave him a thumbs-up sign and gestured toward the pitcher of margaritas I'd brought down on a tray with two glasses, the extra one for Carla on the off chance Mitch got held up. "You pass," I said. "Help yourself."

"Thanks." He picked up Carla's glass, then filled it with my frozen concoction. He took a sip and made a face that suggested pure bliss. I grinned in satisfaction and leaned back, tilting my face up to the sun. Anyone who likes my very bold, decidedly *not* watered-down margaritas is okay in my book.

"I should probably confess something," he said. I turned to the side. "The *Back to the Future* ride is really only my second favorite thing at Universal."

I shifted, propping myself up on my elbow. "Oh? That answer earned you a margarita, bud. I expect some serious explaining."

"Of course," he said, his expression reflecting the seriousness of the moment. "My real favorite ride is the tram ride." He held up a hand as if to halt my protests. "I know. Major Cheez Whiz, but it's just so damn cool. I mean, you get to see the *Psycho* house. How do you beat that?"

Okay, I already knew that I liked this guy, but now I really *liked* him. "You," I said, with an appropriate tone of respect and awe, "may have as much of my margaritas as you want."

"I passed?"

"You totally passed."

"I'm glad," he said. But this time, the casual banter was gone, replaced by a voice that seemed to trill over me, making me shiver despite the relentless rays of the sun.

I took a long sip of margarita, wondering if he'd put that heat into his voice on purpose, and also wanting to quell the the way the warmth had bloomed inside me. I blamed it on the sun and the alcohol. Not my reaction to the guy. After all, I'd already determined that he was a nice guy. And I'd had my fill of nice guys with Dex.

I took a quick glance his direction and was immediately vindicated. He was, I noticed, holding a battered copy of Asimov's *The Robots of Dawn*. For the record, I'm a big fan of Asimov. But so was Dex. And in my experience, guys who read Asimov tend not to be the kind of guys who can provide serious assistance in the sexual satisfaction department. Unscientific, possibly biased. But in Mattie Brown world, that's a fact.

I told myself that was a good thing. Because that sensual little trill I'd felt a few moments ago was a fluke. A mistake. An alcohol-induced reaction. Not real, and certainly nothing to get excited about. Pun totally intended.

Besides, the truth is that there was no way that Mike I-Read-Asimov-And-Ride-The-Tram Peterson could have pulled out all the sexy-voice stops on purpose. I mean, why would he? Since I happened to know that Cullen was on a photo shoot in Aruba until tomorrow (he'd asked me to bring in his mail), I'd gone to the pool wearing no makeup, and decked out in my rattiest bathing suit, threadbare and sun-faded. The one that does *not* create the illusion that I have thin thighs. (For the record, my thighs aren't huge; I know that. But they are disproportioned, or at least I think so. Bigger at the top than oh, say, Kate Moss. Which always makes buying jeans an adventure. At any rate, I've had a love/hate relationship with my thighs since puberty, with the hate part of the equation usually coming out on top.)

This afternoon, I'd thrown caution and thigh camouflage to the wind. Not to mention makeup, hair and a remotely attractive bathing suit. In other words, I wasn't exactly exuding sexuality. But I told myself that that was fine, because Mike wasn't exactly Cullen. Which, to my margarita-soaked mind, put us on pretty equal footing.

I shifted a little, then turned to look more directly at him. I wasn't really sure if he was keen on talking—he might rather read—but he must have caught my vibe because he lowered the book and shot me a winning smile.

"So how are you settling in?"

He put the book aside, giving me his full attention. "Well, the water pressure in the shower stinks, I still can't find my electric razor, the radio from my car's already been stolen and the lady who lives below me seems to think I'm the son she never had." He smiled, a truly infectious grin, and I found myself smiling back. "In other words, a pretty typical move so far."

I laughed. "That's Mrs. Stevenson. She's lived here

since the beginning of time. She's certain she knows who shot JFK, and insists we never actually landed on the moon. But she's harmless and she bakes great chocolate-chip cookies. I highly recommend getting on her good side." Those cookies more than made up for listening to her wild theories at the mailbox.

"I'll keep that in mind." When he grinned, a little dimple appeared in his cheek, and I was struck once again by how cute he was. Not knock-you-down gorgeous hunk-o-man like Cullen. But cute. Like your best guy friend in high school.

"Where'd you move from, anyway?"

"Austin."

"Ah. A cowboy," I teased.

"Hardly. Before that I was in Silicon Valley."

"Then you must be a dot-com guy."

"Something like that. Computer gaming."

"Ooooh."

His eyebrows raised. "Why do you say it like that?"

"I'm not saying it any particular way," I lied.

"Yes, you are. You didn't just say, 'oh, computer games.' You said 'ooooh,' like I'd just solved some mystery of life or something."

"It's just that that's a field I know absolutely nothing about."

That seemed to satisfy him, because he nodded

and said, "It's pretty interesting. Hard work, but interesting."

In truth, I'd just told a big fat lie, but that was okay. Because this was one of those occasions when it's okay to save someone's feelings. Like a guy to whom you would otherwise have to say, *I said 'ooooh,' because you'd just confirmed what I already thought I knew—that you really are the new nerd in residence. Not boy toy material at all. Which is too bad, because you really are a hottie, and I'm having a hard time not reaching out to stroke your chest.*

Okay, yes, that was a little much. And I quelled those thoughts and simply said, "Sounds like you really like it."

"Love it," he said. "Right now I'm heading up a team that's writing the code and the script for a new cutting-edge game. Multiple players, AI interface. It's going to be state of the art."

"Fab," I said, but my enthusiasm was false. Computer games are so not my thing. I played Super Mario Brothers once years ago, lost badly, and was scarred for life. Haven't hooked up an Xbox, Nintendo or logged on to a game site since. Clearly, Mike and I had very little in common.

Too bad a surprising little voice whispered

before I managed to shove it to the back of my brain. Mike was simply not a possibility. I had a plan to up my slut score, and I wasn't going to leap into a repeat of my three years with Dex simply because that plan—not to mention Cullen Slater— made me nervous.

Of course, considering Mike hadn't made any sort of a move, I suppose I was getting ahead of myself….

"So what do you do?" he asked, following the traditionally accepted getting-to-know-you patter.

"I work in a production company. I'm the VP of Business Affairs."

"I'm impressed."

"Don't be." I resisted rolling my eyes. "I got into this job because what I really want to do is write screenplays, and I thought it was an in into the industry."

"It's not?"

"Hardly," I said sourly. "And the worst of it is that I'm working such long hours that I'm usually too exhausted to write." The words rolled off my tongue, surprising me. I desperately wanted to break into screenwriting, true, but I didn't usually go around whining about it to people I've only just met. I told myself to tone it down as I waved vaguely around the pool area. "This weekend is an unexpected bonus."

"That's rough," he said. "But it still sounds interesting. Working in television must be fun."

He sounded genuinely interested. Most people are. Television does that.

I shrugged. "We produce reality shows. You know. The programs that are currently multiplying like locusts on your television lineup."

"Ah, yes. I think I've heard something about those." His mouth twitched, either amused at my definition or my utter lack of loyalty to my profession. My level of guilt, however, was minimal. Reality shows are a scourge. And at the moment, I was still irritated with John.

"Still, you're in the business," Mike said. "Isn't that what L.A.'s all about?"

Okay, I was beginning to really like this guy. He was repeating back to me exactly what I'd told my mother after I'd turned down the law firm position. Not to mention what I told myself every time I felt a twinge about not having yet sold a screenplay. "Exactly."

We shared a smile before he cleared his throat and stood up. "Listen, I've got a pizza in the fridge that just needs to be heated up. I'd love some company."

"Oh. Right. Um." The truth was that I'd love to just hang out with him, but I'd already filled and exceeded my allotment of sluffing off time for the day. My plan had been to simply veg for a bit—to numb my mind with margaritas and sunshine before returning to the equally mind-numbing task of furniture assembly. "I wish I could. But I have a pile of furniture waiting to be assembled." I held up my margarita for emphasis. "I took a break to get in the mood."

"I understand that," he said. "I've schlepped more boxes to the recycling bin than I care to count, and it's a wonder my eyes aren't crossed from reading the assembly instructions on the IKEA shelves I bought."

"Exactly," I said, sensing a kindred spirit. "I mean, who wrote those anyway?"

"Monkeys with typewriters?" He laughed and I laughed, and for a second I thought maybe he'd offer to help me interpret my monkey-written instructions. But instead, he just stood up and gestured to the pitcher. "Thanks for the margarita."

"Oh. Sure." I started to gather my things, unreasonably irritated that he was so casually departing. I told myself I was annoyed by the breakdown of basic good manners. I mean, a chivalrous guy would have offered to help, right? Even Cullen would have offered. That's what guys who look good without their shirts do, right? Offer to engage in manual labor so they have an opportunity to show off their pecs?

Mike, however, wasn't showing off. He was just gathering his things to leave.

"So why are you out here all alone? I usually see you with Carla."

"She declined my distress call for assembly help," I said, giving him one more chance at that whole chivalry thing. "It's okay. I'm well aware of how much she values her manicure."

"Which apartment is hers?"

"Oh, she's not in this building. She's in the complex next door." Our street was lined with apartment complex after apartment complex. "Her building doesn't have a pool or a laundry room," I added, by way of explaining why Carla was almost always here. At least, she was here if Mitch-the-Wonder-Stud wasn't there.

His eyes met mine and he flashed me a zinger of a smile. "I guess that's just one more reason why I'm certain I chose the right complex to move into."

"Um, yeah." For a guy who'd just failed Chivalry 101, he could be pretty damn charming.

"Later," he said, with a small wave.

"Right. Later." I waved goodbye, then watched him head up the staircase while I gathered my things.

As I did, I realized he'd taken my extra glass with him. A little burst of emotion shot through me, and it wasn't irritation.

No, this was anticipation. Because if he had my glass, I'd have to see him again. And that, I thought, wasn't a bad thing at all.

He might not be chivalrous, but he *was* nice. And another friend in the building never hurt.

3

As soon as Mike opened his door, Stephanie greeted him with a wolf whistle. "Cute girl," she said.

"Not your type," Mike said with a grin. "She's a fan of the Y chromosome."

"Damn. Foiled again."

He laughed, shaking his head as he slid into one of the kitchen chairs. He and Stephanie had been best friends since elementary school. They'd gone steady for about a week in eighth grade, which had ruined their friendship until the second semester of their sophomore year. That was when Steph had come to him in tears, desperate to talk about the crush she had on the new girl in school. Mike had listened, dried her tears, and their friendship had continued on, stronger than ever. With the added bonus that they could now discuss their relative girlfriends.

"So is she a new special friend?" Steph asked,

lacing her voice with a tease as she tried to uncork a bottle of wine.

"Friend, yes. Special, definitely. Special friend…" He trailed off with a shrug, then took the bottle and the corkscrew from her, handily freeing the cork. "I'm working on that one."

Steph's eyebrows rose infinitesimally. "Oh, really? Tell me all about it or I withhold the wine."

"I've been drinking margaritas," he said, holding up his now-empty glass. "I'm passing on the wine anyway."

She squinted at the glass, the blown Mexican kind with a bluish tint and a dark blue rim. "One of hers?"

"Yup," he said, mildly proud of himself for walking off with it.

From Steph's grin, he knew she understood. "Cinderella's slipper."

"Exactly. I keep the glass, I have a reason to go back and see her."

Actually, he already had a reason. She'd been hinting hard enough about the furniture assembly. He could have easily stood up, held out his hand, and said, "Come on. Let's go take care of that."

The trouble with that option, though, was that while it would certainly impress her, it wouldn't impress her in a way that fit in his overall plan of attack. Go when she asks, and he's simply some male sap doing her bidding. But go in an hour or so—when she's buried in hardware and frustrated—and suddenly he's the hero. And all the more sexy for it.

"So tell me about her," Steph said, coming to the table with a glass of wine for her and a Coke for him. Mike glanced at the clock, evaluated how much time he had before Mattie hit maximum frustration, and nodded.

"I met her the day I moved in," he said, starting at the beginning. He told Steph the rest of it, too. All of it. From the heat of desire he felt when he looked at Mattie to the secret plan he'd overheard in the laundry room.

Steph took it all in without saying a word. He knew she understood the depth of his emotion. Mike wasn't the type to fall hard and fast, but he was the kind to believe in love at first sight. His parents had seen each other from across a lecture hall as freshmen in college, and had been gloriously in love ever since. His family was close-knit, and unlike so many families these days, "family" included all the various extensions, including especially his grandparents.

Grandma Jo and Grandpa Fred had moved in across the street when Mike was eight. He'd grown up in the thrall of family, and he knew that he was stronger for it. More, because his grandparents' relationship was just as strong as his parents'—and had happened just as quickly—Mike had always craved a deep love and a long-term relationship. Silly, perhaps, to base personal dreams on the love life of his family members, but Mike saw how happy his parents and grandparents were.

He'd explained all that to Steph years ago. And she knew better than anyone that Mike had yet to find his perfect woman. So for him to be so frazzled so quickly…well, that was saying a lot.

He described Mattie and her plan, and when he was finished, Steph leaned back in the chair, nodded slowly, and simply said, "Interesting."

"That's it? I tell you that the first woman who's really sparked my interest in the last year is looking to ratchet up her sex life, and all you can say is *interesting?* How about 'Wow, what an opportunity you've stumbled across?' Or 'Gee, what lucky star were you born under?'"

"Or maybe 'Boy, have you got your work cut out for you,'" she said, looking at him gravely.

"You're kidding, right?" he said, wondering what had possessed her to be so negative.

She rolled her eyes. "Mike, you used to be a lot less naive. Or am I wrong about your intentions here?"

"My intentions," he said, feeling utterly old-fashioned, "are completely honorable."

"Well, that's the rub, isn't it? She's looking for a wild fling. A bit of experience between the sheets. She said her ex was a dud, right? That means she's looking for a good time. And she's *not* looking for commitment."

He frowned; she had a point.

"And did she come on to you at the pool?" Steph pressed. Mike had to admit that she hadn't. "Well, there you go."

He held out his hands, hoping he demonstrated just how much he didn't understand what she was talking about.

Steph sighed and rolled her eyes. "Straight guys are just plain dumb," she said. "*Obviously,* she already has someone in mind to play stud."

"Or she's just not attracted to me."

Steph shook her head. "No way," she said, loyally. "You're irresistible." She crossed her arms over her chest and cocked her head. "No, the only reason our little friend wasn't playing Flirt Girl with you is that she's saving up for someone else. So your job, my friend, is to convince her she's got her eye on the wrong guy."

"Uh-huh," he said, beginning to wonder if he wouldn't have been better off keeping his mouth shut.

"And exactly how am I supposed to do that? Chocolate? Roses? Get her drunk and screw her brains out?"

"Not a bad plan," Steph said, without skipping a beat. "But I think your best approach is to just ease your way into her life. Find out who she's going after. And then make sure you're in position to fill in the gaps if her plan stumbles."

"And why would it stumble?" he asked.

"Who knows why these things go awry? But if she's already in the mind frame of seduction. And if you're already in her life. Well, then, wouldn't her natural reaction be to turn to you?"

"You're devious. You know that, right?"

"Oh yeah," she said. "I know. The question is, am I right?"

He thought about that. About getting close to her. About the fact that Mattie Brown was the kind of woman he'd enjoy hanging out with. Talking with. Taking long walks with. And, of course, he'd enjoy running his hands over her naked body and driving her positively wild. *That* was a given.

But the friendship aspect? Yeah, he wanted that, too. And if by being her friend, he could be her lover…

His fingertip slowly traced the rim of the margarita glass. "Yeah," he said slowly, after he'd thought it all over. "Yeah, I think you're right."

I HATE PRESSBOARD. THAT fake wood with veneer on it filled with packed sawdust that weighs umpteen million pounds.

So far, I'd managed to chip the corners of two pieces, strip the screw-hole out of a third piece, and mutilate my toe by dropping yet another piece right on it. All in the name of a lateral filing cabinet I didn't want for a job I didn't want.

Honestly.

And I was all the more irritated because my sister had called earlier, just to say "Hi," she'd said. But when I'd told her about my furniture dilemma, she'd immediately launched into a narrative about how *her* boss had insisted she not work at home. He wants her to have a life, he said. And to make sure she was comfortable whenever she did have to work long hours at the office, he gave her an astronomical furniture budget and told her to go for it.

Even in furniture, Angie wins out. I tell you, it's enough to drive a girl batty.

I shoved thoughts of my sister out of my head, and instead focused on the mess in front of me. What I needed was help. Immediately, an image of Mike filled my head. Nice Mike. Cute Mike. Mike with the awesome upper body.

I shook myself. *Bad Mattie. Bad. Bad.*

Still…I did need to get that margarita glass back. And if he asked me what I was doing—and if I told him I was having a heck of a time assembling some furniture—and if he offered to help me out…well, who was I to say no?

Having thus justified seeing him one more time, I stood and headed to the door. I paused to check my face and hair in the mirror I keep hanging there, decided I looked respectable if not awesome, and pulled open the door to reveal the man himself.

"Mike! I was just coming to see you!"

He held up my margarita glass. "Desperate to get it back?"

"No, of course not," I said, even though that had totally been my planned excuse. "I, um, was hoping you could give me a hand." I stepped back from the door and ushered him in.

He brushed past me, glanced around, then turned to face me directly. "Don't take this the wrong way, but did a sawmill erupt in here?"

"Very funny." I plucked the glass out of his hand. "Will you help me if I offer to fill this back up for you?"

He flashed me a grin, charming, but with a hint of mischief. "With an offer like that, how could I refuse?"

Since I'm not a fool, I immediately slapped an Allen wrench into his open palm and pointed him toward the instructions (balled up under the television stand where I'd kicked them in a fit of pique.) He scored points by not even looking at me funny as he bent to dig them out.

I retreated to the kitchen to make the margaritas.

Not that *retreated* really describes it. The apartment is only about seven hundred square feet consisting of a big rectangle filled with a living area, a dining area and a kitchen area, pretty much all open to each other unless you're standing way back by the fridge.

Between the dining area (carpeted) and the kitchen area (tiled) were two stairs leading up to a tiny bathroom on the left and a decent-size bedroom on the right. That's it. End of grand tour.

It's not much, but you'd think differently if you saw the check I wrote every month. Studio City doesn't come cheap.

All of which is to say that even though I couldn't see Mike the whole time, I could hear him. And it felt nice and cozy—and scarily domestic—to be working in the kitchen while he was shuffling pieces of wood and muttering to himself.

Since making margaritas requires little more than dumping ice and alcohol into a blender and pressing On, it didn't take me too long to whip up a batch. Even so, in the short time that I was gone, Mike had managed to assemble an entire base section of the cabinet.

"Wow. You're good." I handed him his drink then sat on the floor next to him, looking at what he'd accomplished in only a few minutes, compared to the nothing I'd accomplished in hours.

"Call it a guy thing," he said, then he flashed that grin again. I really like that grin, and I felt my stomach do one of those flip-flop numbers.

I turned away, suddenly feeling shy. "So, um, what can I do to help?"

"Just keep bringing the margaritas. I've got a handle on everything else."

"And you're sure you don't mind?"

He looked up at me, and I felt warm and tingly all over. More, I knew that he was telling me the absolute truth when he said, "No. I don't mind at all."

And so that's how it happened. He worked and I sat there watching him. Watching and sipping and serving margaritas as the two of us got more and more tipsy.

"So how come the sudden need for new furniture?" he asked later. By this time he'd finished assembling (in about one-bazillionth of the time it would have taken me), and was kicked back, leaning against my new cabinet, a margarita loose in his hand.

Technically we still barely knew each other. But we'd spent the last hour chatting in close quarters, and there was something about him that made me feel as though we were old friends. It was a nice feeling; one I hadn't experienced with a guy since high school, actually. And I told him the ins and outs of my job. "I know I have a good deal, so I hate to gripe. I mean, my checking account is nice and full. But my ideas? They're starting to dwindle. It's like I'm losing touch with some spark of creativity."

I took in a breath and let it out slowly. "It's scary. But being jobless is scarier still. Especially if you were raised in a family like mine where the mighty paycheck is king, the power job is emperor and social prestige is God himself."

He watched me intently while I told all of this. Not in a way that made me uncomfortable, but as if everything I had to say was important. And when I finished, he was nodding a little. "I know exactly what you're going through," he said. "It took all my courage to quit my day job and start freelancing. Hardest thing I've done in my life."

"But it's paid off for you," I said. "Right?"

"Absolutely." He'd told me earlier a bit about what he does—designing computer games and writing the script for them and everything—and he'd become less geeky in my eyes. I mean, writing scripts was what *I* wanted to do.

"So do you think I'm being a coward?" I asked. At the same time, I wasn't entirely sure I wanted an answer. I realized that I valued his opinion. If he did think I was foolish for sticking it out with John, what would that mean? Because I didn't think I had the courage to chuck it with John Layman Productions. Not yet. Maybe not ever. But at the same time, the thought of Mike thinking I was acting like an idiot bothered me a lot more than I'd expected. Or, honestly, wanted to admit.

Lucky for me, he didn't criticize. Instead, he just said that everyone has a different path to get where they want to be. "So long as you can see the path— and so long as you don't let that creative spark die— then you're on track. But at the same time, you have to keep your eyes open for places where the path veers. Otherwise, you could end up missing the exit that leads to the job you really want."

"Love the highway analogy," I said, teasing. But I was happy he hadn't called me a fool. I kept my thoughts to myself, though, because *I* was calling myself an idiot and a fool and a coward. I'd stopped seeing the path long ago, and had been working simply for a paycheck for years. That burning desire to sell a screenplay was still burning in my gut, but it was as if I was stymied in how to go about it. Burning out from the inside. The idea terrified me, and yet I didn't know how to turn the situation around.

I didn't tell Mike that, though, for fear he'd think less of me. And for reasons I didn't want to analyze, I really wanted him to see me in a good light.

So I did what I always do when I want to avoid an issue—I changed the subject.

"Well," I said, standing up, "you've earned your margarita by assembling the thing, but if you want to earn a meal to go with it, you're going to have to put some muscle into it."

"Yeah?" he said, grinning at the challenge in my voice.

"Doesn't do me much good in the middle of my living room," I said. "And I'm too weak and fragile a female to move it all by myself."

That earned me a guffaw, and I liked him even more.

"Okay," I admitted. "Not weak and fragile, but slightly tipsy and definitely lazy. Does the code of chivalry require that knights come to the aid of drunken maidens?"

"Absolutely," he said. "So long as the knight is equally drunk."

"I guess you qualify, then."

He downed the last few ounces of his margarita, his eyes never leaving mine. "Yes, ma'am. I guess I do."

"Right." I cleared my throat, fighting the warm fuzzy feeling growing in my tummy, and trying to convince myself it was alcohol induced and not related to the man. He was, I reminded myself, perfectly good friend material. But for a slot on my boyfriend list? Nope. Not a possibility. Mike was far too Dex-like, and that was a well I didn't intend to drink from again.

"So," I continued. "Um, how about moving it over there?" I pointed toward my very cluttered desk and the space on my floor now occupied with scraps of paper related to various John Layman Productions. And, of course, a dozen fan magazines. Won't do for a Layman exec not to know all about the up-and-coming celebs.

While Mike got a grip on the cabinet, I scurried over and shoved all that detritus out of the way. He hoisted the thing himself, turning down my request to give him a hand, then worked it across the room.

"Wow," I said, once it was in place. "You're a handy guy to have around."

"Lucky for you I live right across the hall," he said.

"Yeah," I said, feeling warm all over. "Very lucky."

Our eyes met, and it was one of those moments you read about in romance novels. Unfortunately, I didn't want that kind of moment because he was *friend*—not *fling*—material. So I cleared my throat and looked away, and then he did the same, and suddenly we were out of romance novel land and into the world of awkward reality.

Gee, what an improvement. Not.

When he'd turned from me, he'd ended up facing my desktop, and now he pointed at a stack of papers. "What's this?"

I peered toward him and saw the pile of Cullen's mail. Immediately, I blushed. Stupid, because Mike couldn't know (at least not for sure) that I thought he was cute or was fighting warm fuzzies in my tummy. And he also couldn't know that I thought Cullen was hot, and I was currently concocting a plan for nailing him.

But stupid or not, I blushed, and then I stammered as I covered, explaining that I was bringing in the mail for our neighbor who was off in Aruba at the moment.

"Right," Mike said, nodding thoughtfully. "The guy who lives there." He pointed to my western wall. "He's some sort of model?"

I nodded and shrugged at the same time, trying to

convey careless indifference. I also tried not to look at Mike, but I didn't do a very good job. I don't know why I suddenly felt so ridiculous—as if the idea of trying to hook up with Cullen was the goofiest idea ever conceived on the planet—but I did. And I felt all the more embarrassed because Mike was there to see me wallow in my own idiocy.

Honestly, the man was wreaking havoc with my emotions. And my confidence. And my self-control.

If he was going to be my friend—and I really did want him to be—I was going to have to learn to pull myself together. At the very least, I was going to have to avoid alcohol around him. I mean, surely it was the margaritas making me so stupid. What else could it be?

I realized he was looking at me, his expression thoughtful, as if I were a puzzle he'd just solved. I wasn't sure I liked that, so I got up and started moving around, wishing I could take back the last few minutes. He got up, too, and I had the odd feeling that he wanted to rewind, as well.

I started gathering all the various tools and bits of trash left over from the assembly project, and after a few seconds Mike bent down to help me. "You keep feeding me margaritas," he said. "I feel like I should do something in return."

I gestured at the file cabinet. "Um, I think you did."

"You're right," he said dryly. "You still owe me big-time."

I laughed. "True enough. How can I pay up?" The second I said the words, I regretted them. There'd been something buzzing in the air between us earlier, but I really wanted to ignore that.

"I could use some assembly-type help myself," he said. "Maybe tomorrow evening?"

"You're kidding, right? You saw the mess when you got here. If you need something demolished, I'm your girl. Assembled, not so much."

"What I need is someone to help me hang some shelves. Takes about three hands, and unfortunately, I've only got two. All you'll have to do is stand where I tell you and hold something still. I think even you can handle that," he added wryly.

"Oh, thanks. Thanks a lot."

We shared a quick grin, and then he said, very casually, "I'm also a whiz at ordering pizza, so I'm happy to feed you. And maybe we could watch a movie, too." He pointed to one of the framed movie posters I have hanging in the corner by my desk, this one of William Powell and Myrna Loy in *The Thin Man*. "I take it you're a fan of classic movies?"

"Oh yeah. And especially *The Thin Man* series.

Sophisticated comedy. They just don't make them like that anymore."

"No, they don't," he said, a little distractedly. "Why don't we watch that movie?"

"The Thin Man?" I asked. "That would be terrific. I heard they finally released it on DVD, but I haven't gotten around to buying it. Are you a fan? Do you have a copy?"

"Oh, yeah," he said, looking at the poster instead of at me. "It's such a great movie. Couldn't live without owning it. So if you want, we could relax after our labors and watch the movie. What do you say? You game?"

I looked at him, just standing there all casual, one neighbor to another. He was only asking me to hang shelves, after all, not have sex. (A little voice in my head said that was a very unfortunate oversight, but I managed to shut that voice up quickly.)

I knew I should say no. After all, I had a hell of a lot on my plate. The demands of my job, for example. Not to mention the stress associated with figuring out how to seduce my neighbor.

But when I thought of all that stress, the first thing that popped into my mind was how nice it would be to hang out with Mike, eat pizza, and watch Nick and Nora—not to mention Asta—solve a mystery.

So I said yes. And as soon as I did, I realized it was the right thing to say.

And, honestly, that scared me just a little.

4

RING, RING.

Me: Hello. (Translation: *"Hello."*)

Mom: Mattie? (Translation: *"I hope you're awake, dear, it's after dawn."*)

Me: Hi, Mom. What's up? (*"Why are you calling me at this God-awful hour on a Sunday?"*)

Mom: I'm not interrupting anything, am I? (*"I expect you to be up and working by six. The weekends are no reason to slack off!"*)

Me: Nope. Not doing a thing. (*"I'm belatedly exercising my right to teenage rebellion!"*)

Mom: One of our first years transferred to Boston. We have an opening in the real estate division. I could pull a few strings. (*"I don't want to let a week pass without reminding you that you completely disappointed me by turning your back on such a noble profession."*)

Me: I really appreciate the offer, Mom. (*"I'd*

rather rip my toenails out.") But things are going great for me (*"Liar! Liar!"*), and I'm not ready to throw in the towel. (*"And even if I were, I'd rather work at Starbucks than share office space with my maternal unit."*)

Mom: You're not getting any younger. (*"You're three years from thirty! Why haven't you conquered the world yet?"*)

Me: I know, Mom. (*"Please, let's change the subject."*)

Mom: How is that boyfriend of yours? Rex? (*"Nice guy. Forgettable." On that, at least, we agree.*)

Me: We broke up months ago. (*"Would it kill you to actually listen to your daughter once in a while?"*)

Mom: Oh. Well, I'm sorry. (*"How inconvenient to have forgotten key information. I must remember to take my Gingko."*)

Me: I've got to run. (*"Get me out of here!"*)

Mom: You be good. (*"Don't catch anything embarrassing from those unwashed Hollywood types you associate with."*)

Me: I'll try. (*"Oh, shit. Condoms."*)

"CONDOMS."

Carla nearly spit nonfat latte down the front of her blouse, but recovered nicely. "Excuse me?"

"Dex and I were tested. I'm on birth control pills. I haven't done the condom thing in over three years." I'd been thinking about this for hours. Obsessing, really. I mean, it's not as though the whole in-the-moment condom thing comes naturally. So it was sort of like the giant hippopotamus in the living room when, really, I had a long list of other, more important things to obsess about. (Not the least of which was how to have even the tiniest of chances with— *oh my God!*—Cullen Slater.)

Carla just waved a hand, apparently unconcerned over my angst. "Honey, it's just like riding a bicycle."

The waiter-dude—very tan, very blond—came over to top off my coffee and deliver our bagels. I waited an appropriate interval before jumping back into the whole condom quagmire.

"The thing of it is, I never really got past the training wheels stage." I could feel myself blush, and took a quick sip of coffee in a feeble attempt to keep Carla from noticing.

Didn't work. "Training wheels?" She cocked her head in that very Carla way she has, then used her fork to capture the tiniest bite of cream cheese imaginable even as she kept me under scrutiny. "Explain, please."

Perk Up! is a cramped little dive on Ventura Boulevard, just two blocks from my Studio City apartment. It's also extremely popular—especially on a Sunday morning—and the owners are no dummies. Any closer together and the tiny tables would be stacked. I leaned over and lowered my voice. "I was never very good at getting it on…you know…on *it.*"

Carla rolled her eyes. "If you can't say it, you can't do it."

"Well, I guess that explains my pathetic eighteen percent, doesn't it? Happy?" I wasn't. Me and my flaming cheeks would have crawled under the table right then except that, with such a teeny table, under wasn't an option.

"I'm not anywhere near as happy as you'll be when you get Cullen Slater between the sheets." Her brow wrinkled. "Except I'm not completely sure he's a doing-it-in-the-bed kind of guy. Not that that would be a problem…"

I put on my professional face, trying to regroup. "One, I'm sure a bed will be involved at some point. Two, you're happily involved with a great guy and don't need to be drooling over Cullen Slater."

"True enough. I got seventy-five percent on that test. Mitch and I are doing just fine."

I balked. Seventy-five percent? And I got a lousy

eighteen? How could that be? I'd gone out more in high school. And in college, too. True, I never really *did* much of anything, but surely Carla wasn't out having a wild time while I'd been cramming for a calculus final. Was she?

No, Carla's superior score came from three years of dating Mitch the Wonder Stud, while I'd probably lost points because of my wasted years with Dex. My years with sweet, boring Dex had earned me a whopping eighteen percent.

I took my frustration out on my bagel, smearing cream cheese on with violent exuberance. Then I shoveled in a jumbo-size bite and tried (mostly unsuccessfully) to chew.

"We're getting off the subject," I said, after I'd finally managed to swallow. "I need help. Seventy-five percent kind of help. So guess who's elected?"

"To do what?"

I pulled my notebook out of my backpack and flipped to the page with my notes on what skills I needed so I wouldn't embarrass myself. After all, I lived next door to the man. If I was lousy in bed, there's no way I could face him every day. I'd have to move. And it's hell finding a good apartment in Studio City. I turned the notebook around for Carla while I studied my handwriting upside down, using the end of my fork to point.

"I figure I'm okay with kissing—"

"You're not testing that theory on me."

I rolled my eyes. "I've never gotten any complaints. But…well…" I tried to figure out how to put it delicately. "I guess I just don't have much of a repertoire."

Carla nodded sagely. "I see the problem," she said, then laid a mentorish hand on mine. "And I can help." A slightly goofy smile zipped across her lips, then disappeared. "In fact, I think I can help more than you know."

I scowled, not sure if she was being serious, sarcastic or ironic. I decided not to worry about the possibilities and said simply, "But can you help me *now?*"

"Absolutely. And I know just where to start." She took a sip of her latte, then aimed a beatific smile at me. "Toys."

"Excuse me?" I pictured a giant stuffed bear sitting in front of a Nintendo game. Probably not what she had in mind.

"You need variety. You need toys. And you need something…um…anatomically correct to practice the whole condom thing on." She smiled, big-sisterly, flaunting her two months of seniority over me. "Make a list sweetie. I'm taking you shopping."

To Buy:
- Diet Coke
- Bread
- Condoms—plain, ribbed, *colored*
- Peanut Butter—crunchy and creamy
- Wine—red and white
- Candles
- K-Y
- Cap'n Crunch
- Milk
- Eggs
- Underwear—thongs? lace? crotchless?
- Picante sauce
- Vibrator—what size? Do vibrators have sizes?
- Potato chips
- Coffee
- Beer

MIKE HAD SPENT THE MORNING on the phone, quickly learning that many video stores didn't open until eleven on Sunday. He switched to the Internet, and made a list of all the stores in the area that sold DVDs. Then he puttered around his apartment, trying to concentrate on the news channel he'd turned on— or at least focus on not burning his toast—but he wasn't having much luck with either.

Why had he told Mattie that he owned *The Thin Man?* And worse, if he was going to tell her such a bold fib, why hadn't he at least allowed himself a day or two to track down the thing? What was he supposed to say when she came over tonight to help him hang shelves if he couldn't find a copy of the DVD to buy? That he'd misplaced it? That a thief had broken in and stolen his collection of classic movies? That he sucked at thinking on his feet when the woman beside him was scrambling his brain? Or, more honestly, when he was laboring under a fit of intense jealousy at the thought of Mattie pursuing Cullen Slater?

And that, really, was the rub. He didn't know for certain, of course, but considering the way she'd blushed when he'd pointed to Cullen's mail, Mike figured it was reasonable to assume that Cullen was the centerpiece in Mattie's plan to enrich her sexual vocabulary. And, honestly, Mike hated the other man for that.

Stupid, he knew, since Cullen most likely had no idea that he was the focus of Mattie's plans. But Mike wasn't in the habit of arguing with his emotions. No, his temperament leaned much more toward the scientific and methodical. Mattie was aiming for an outcome that paired her with Cullen. Mike didn't like that outcome. In order to alter the outcome, Mike needed to alter the ultimate equation. Q.E.D.

But, of course, it wasn't all that simple. For one thing, the only change he was interested in making put *him* into the equation in place of Cullen. Fine in theory, but much harder in practice—as evidenced by the fact that he'd now gotten himself into quite a bind by pretending he owned *The Thin Man.*

And he hadn't stopped there! Oh, no. In a fit of utter stupidity, he'd gone on to tell her that he was a fan of the classic movie. Too bad for him he'd never seen the thing.

Not only was he a pathetic liar, but he was a pathetic liar who needed to take a crash course in *The Thin Man,* starting with who starred in the damn thing. And, of course, what the movie was about!

He realized he'd been pacing while holding a glass of orange juice and that, so far, he hadn't take a sip. He glanced at the clock, saw that it was after eleven, and decided he might as well start his movie quest. After all, he only had a few short hours until the evening, and during that time he needed to find and buy the DVD, learn a bit of history about the movie—and watch it at least once so that it was familiar—and buy the shelves that Mattie was coming over to help him hang.

Honestly, it would be a miracle if he was done by midnight. Too bad he only had until seven.

He grabbed his keys, then headed out the door and to the parking area. He'd try the video stores on Ventura Boulevard first, and if those were a bust he'd start calling stores on his cell phone until he found one with the movie in stock.

Since his apartment was only two blocks from Ventura, it took him no time to get there. He was idling in front of the newsstand at the intersection of Laurel Canyon and Ventura when he looked up and saw Mattie and Carla come out of Perk Up! and start walking down the street. About the same time his light turned green, he saw them climb into a cherry-red PT Cruiser.

He'd been planning on going right, but the devil who'd taken up permanent residence on his shoulder urged him to turn left instead, much to the chagrin of the elderly lady in the car behind him.

He made the turn, then kept his speed to a crawl until he was alongside the Cruiser. Carla was driving, which didn't surprise him, and the girls were chattering, so engrossed in their conversation that he was sure they hadn't noticed him.

Good. Because he hadn't a clue what he'd say if Mattie caught his eye and then asked what he was doing. How could he answer when he didn't even know himself?

He drove as slowly as he dared, and—*finally*—Carla passed him. He exhaled, relieved, and pulled in behind her, careful to keep a bit of distance. A little trill ran through him, despite the fact that he was fully aware he was acting like an adolescent. But the fact was, no woman in years had made him *want* to act like an adolescent. So while the behavior might be on the absurd side, the emotion—that sense of wonder and longing and desire—filled and buoyed him...and more than made up for the fact that he was currently trailing the woman he'd developed a serious crush on.

He drove in a haze for the next few miles, then had to change lanes quickly when Carla pulled into a strip shopping center. She parked a few doors down from a video store—one he'd been intending to check out, actually—and he sank down in the front seat, hoping neither girl noticed him.

They didn't.

They were too busy heading into The Pleasure Palace three doors down. It was, Mike knew, a famous sex-toy shop. And the idea of Mattie browsing among the leather and rubber and scented gels and oils sent a sudden shot of heat coursing through him.

This had to be about Mattie and her ridiculous Cullen-quest. He knew that, and it bothered him.

But at the same time, the thought of Mattie in that store, shopping for a variety of sensual delights... Well, about *that,* he couldn't help but be very, very intrigued.

Knowledge, he knew, was power. This extra insight into Mattie's plan might just give him the extra edge that he needed to get her between his sheets rather than Cullen's.

The question, of course, was how.

"THE PLEASURE PALACE?" I read the very pink, very ornate sign on the door and turned to stare at Carla. "What is this place?"

Carla just shot me a look. That was okay. I didn't really need an answer. And as soon as we stepped through the door, I *really* didn't need an answer. One look around gave me all the information I needed, and I'm pretty sure I was blushing right down to my toes.

The Palace was in Van Nuys, which made sense, I suppose, since Van Nuys used to be the hub of the porn industry. Hell, maybe it still was. I didn't know, and I hoped we wouldn't be finding out. All I wanted was to acquire my various slut accoutrements, and head back to the safety of my living room to figure out what the heck to do with my new toys.

Except, of course, I hadn't yet acquired any toys. In fact, all I was doing was standing in the window, trying to work up the courage to face the store's staff and whatever other customers happened to be around. That's me: slut extraordinaire.

Of course, if I hadn't been standing in the window, I wouldn't have seen Mike. But I did. I saw him not three doors down, walking out of his car and into a video store—the kind that rents and sells movies (not porn, thank goodness; my own debauchery was all I could handle at the moment).

Except, right at the moment, I wasn't even handling my own debauchery very well.

Carla stepped up behind me. "Either your mind is elsewhere or you're going to buy penis-shaped breath mints."

I looked down and realized that I was standing in front of the novelty candy display. I ignored that fact and pointed out the window. "Mike," I said simply. That was enough, Carla leaned forward, craning her neck just in time to see the door to the video store shut behind him.

"So?"

"So! It's *Mike*."

"And," Carla said slowly, "again I say, so?

Unless you think he saw you come in here. And even then, so what?"

I ran my fingers through my hair. "No, I don't think he saw us. But, yeah, what if he did? I mean, what will he think?"

"That you're buying sex toys?"

"Yes, but that's not *me*."

Carla did one of her sighing numbers. The kind where the shoulders rise and fall and she exhales an amazing amount of air. "I didn't think this was about being you," Carla said. "I thought the whole point was that you're unhappy with you."

"I am," I said. Then I frowned. "I mean, not really. It's just, I don't know…" I trailed off, completely miserable. Then I leaned forward and whispered— as if anyone in that store cared what I had to say anyway. "I guess I'm just feeling like an idiot, you know? I mean, going all out to seduce Cullen Slater just because I bombed some Internet Slut Test? That's so…so…"

"Over the top?" Carla put in helpfully.

"Yes! Exactly. It just all seems a bit much."

"I think you want over the top," Carla said, and that twinkle in her eyes that I'd noticed in the coffee shop was back. And I still had no clue what she was thinking. I didn't have time to ask, either, because she went on. "I think over the top is exactly what you need, frankly. Over the top gets you noticed. Big strokes. Broad gestures. The kind of stuff folks talk about around the water cooler the next day."

"Thank you very much, but I am *so* not interested in being office gossip."

"What about being Monday night programming?"

I squinted at her, now completely lost. Carla, however, was far from lost. Her smile was so wide and so bright it competed with the fluorescents that illuminated the dildo display ten feet to our left.

"Carla," I said suspiciously. "What's going on?"

"You," she said. "On television." It was like opening a floodgate. The second she said the word *television,* words started spilling out, as if it had taken Herculean strength to keep her mouth closed. "After we talked yesterday, Timothy happened to call. And we got to talking about one of his new projects, and I mentioned you—"

"You mentioned my sex life to *your boss?*" I couldn't believe she'd do that!

"Yes, but I had a good reason."

I glared at her. "I can't imagine any reason that will get you off the hook with me for something like that!"

"Not even a screenplay sale?"

I blinked. "Explain, please."

Her face was lit with excitement. "You know what cool ideas Timothy comes up with, right? Well, his most recent thing is to do a series of dramas that are loosely based on real life. The shows would be an hour long, but then after the show, he'd air a thirty minute interview show with the writer. Sort of like a whole new spin on reality television, you know?"

I did know, and it sounded brilliant. A lot more enticing than the stuff that my boss came up with!

"Anyway, on a whim I pitched him your whole slut thing. You know, as an idea for the show. I didn't tell him it was you—well, not at first—but when it turned out that he *loves* it, I did tell him it was you. Because, you know, I talk about you and he knows that you can write."

My head was spinning, and I didn't want to jump to any conclusions, so I just stood there, kind of gaping.

"Mattie!" Carla squealed. "Don't you get it? He *loves* the idea! Especially since Cullen has some celebrity appeal. He wants you to write it up and then you'll be the interviewee for the *very first show!* And the best part is that if he likes the television script you know he'll read any movie script you bring to him. It's no guarantee, but he's definitely got the clout to get a picture green-lighted."

"Oh my gosh," I said slowly. Then I squealed, too. "Oh! My! Gosh!" I threw my arms around her and hugged her. This was amazing! Carla was right; it was exactly the kind of break that I needed. Except…

I pulled away. "Do I really want to air out all my personal weirdness?" I could just see Angie smugly sitting back in her Beverly Hills living room and raking in the kudos for being the only sane daughter in the family. *Not* a pretty picture.

Carla laughed. "That's the beauty of it. No one will really believe it's true, and even if they do, so what? It makes good television. It will make you marketable. But you do have to make it good. And that's why I said that—"

"Over the top is even better." I nodded, understanding washing over me. *Could* I do this? Air out my slutlessness on national television, along with my efforts to nail Cullen? Yes, I realized, I could. Considering how I felt lately about getting nowhere in my career working at JLP, I was more than willing to put a little pride on the line if that was necessary to get a break in my career.

"Wow," I said, as I thought the whole thing over. "Wow."

"So?" Carla prodded.

"Yeah," I said. "I'll do it."

"Brilliant," she said. She nodded toward the video

store where we'd seen Mike only minutes before. "Then quit worrying what your mother and your sister and the neighbors will think and let's get on with our shopping. We have a plan to set in motion."

"Right," I said. But I will admit, I took one last look toward the video store, my thoughts lingering on Mike until I'd turned around and found myself faced with a colorful display of dildos and vibrators.

I felt my eyes go wide, and beside me, Carla started chuckling.

"You're really enjoying this, aren't you?"

"Watching totally together Mattie Brown squirm? Oh, yeah. I'm having a blast."

Frowning, I put my sunglasses on, craving anonymity. I'd have to get over that, of course, if this became part of a television episode. But I figured I didn't have to overcome my shyness (or would that be mortification?) all at once. After all, even if Timothy did end up buying my script, we'd have months before any interview aired.

In the meantime, I figured I was entitled to the dark glasses. Not that I expected to see anyone I knew. And, of course, I planned on paying with credit, which pretty much blew the whole anonymous plan to smithereens. Didn't matter. I shoved the glasses more firmly up my nose, took a deep breath, and stepped into the aisle. "Ready."

Let me just say right now that this place was nothing like what I'd been expecting. I'd spent the whole drive anticipating men in dirty raincoats, dim lighting and the funky smell of sweaty leather. Instead, we were in the Gap meets Sex Toys.

Everything was brightly lit, laid out for all to see, and organized by type. Massage oils here, condoms there, unidentifiable plastic rings with a bunch of little bumps near the door. Curious, I sidled over. Except for the hole in the middle, the pink plastic gizmos looked like knobby soap rests.

I gingerly picked one up with two fingers and squinted through the center. Too large to be a thumb-ring, too small for a guy's…well, you know.

Carla poked her head over my shoulder. "It's for a guy. He wears it on…you know."

I felt absurdly grateful that she couldn't say it either, but I didn't believe her. "No way. It's tiny. What kind of guys do they expect to shop here?" I shot a quick glance toward the multipierced college kid working the cash register, but he seemed completely uninterested in our debate. "Midget sex toys?"

"Seriously. It goes on…before…and then—"

"Oh!" I tossed it back into the bin and wiped my hands on my jeans. "I get it."

"Sure you don't want one?" Carla asked, a tease in her voice. "The little bumps face out, and it's supposed to feel awesome."

"Supposed to? You've never, uh, used one?"

She shook her head.

"In that case, I must not need one to hit seventy-five percent." I waved toward the remaining aisles. "Let's move along."

"Right," Carla said, all businesslike. She veered to the left, heading straight for the main counter, her head held high in typical Carla-esque you-can't-shock-me posture.

I followed a few steps behind, keeping my head down and praying no one talked to me.

The checkout counter consisted of a glass case with three display shelves. I gawked at the pink, purple and flesh-colored vibrators lined up like so many cakes in a bakery window, all priced and ready for purchase. The women of L.A. might only buy designer clothes, but their vibrators were decidedly off the rack.

The whole situation left me feeling wild and decadent. Grown-up. Yet even as I was wallowing in adulthood, one tiny part of me still felt like a twelve-year-old sneaking a peek at the pages of *Playgirl*.

Trying for nonchalance, I pushed aside a basket of lubrication samples—in a variety of pastel packages—and leaned over the counter to get a better look. Big mistake. My new posture put me face-to-*whatever* with a hot pink, lifelike vibrator, which, according to the little sign, was charmingly named the Bare Necessity.

I stifled a giggle and pointed.

Our multipierced host smiled blandly. "Something I can help you with?"

"Is that a *bear?*"

He nodded. "It's a really popular model." With a flourish, he reached into the case, grabbed the thing, and plunked it on top of the counter.

I leaned in closer, and Carla did the same. Sure enough, what we had here was your basic lifelike rubber vibrator—except for the hot pink, of course—topped with a pink bear.

Overcome with curiosity, I poked it. Cool to the touch, it shimmied like superhard Jell-O. The little bear—a friendly looking guy with something in its mouth—was crouched at the base of the shaft, as if ready to leap from just over Vibrator Man's balls onto…well, the rest of him.

"He's eating a fish," I said stupidly, realizing that we were staring at a salmon-catching bear poised over a hot pink river of lust. Basically, the Discovery Channel run amok.

"It's the deluxe model," our ever-helpful clerk said. "Spreads out the sensation." Then he reached under and brought out a fishless version. "This one's more concentrated," he said, poking the bear's snout.

"Oh." It was all I could think of to say, since I had no idea what he was talking about.

"Can you turn it on?" Carla never buys anything without a test drive.

He flipped a switch near the base of the superdeluxe version, and Carla experimentally pressed her finger against the fish. Then she repeated the whole process with the fishless model. "*Ooohhh*. Very interesting." She turned to me, a tiny little smile on her face and a gleam in her eye. "Try it."

I did, and was rewarded with a nice gentle vibration against the tip of my finger.

"And you can adjust the speed," the clerk said, ooching the controls up a bit.

I pulled my finger away, frowning. So far, I hadn't figured out how wildlife played into this whole self-gratification scenario.

I wasn't keen on displaying my lack of ignorance, but since these things apparently didn't come with instructions, I sucked up my courage. "What exactly does the—" I snapped my mouth shut, suddenly realizing just where the little bear and his fish would be if I were to insert Part A into Slot Me. "Oh! Right."

"Get it?" Carla asked.

I nodded, beginning to clue in as to why I only scored a measly eighteen percent.

"Would you like to try it?" The guy held the entire contraption out to me, and I took an involuntary step backward. To his credit, he didn't even smirk. Most likely, he dealt with both the exceedingly bold and the exceedingly meek on a daily basis.

Carla—of the exceedingly bold—stepped up and took hold of the thing, testing its weight in her hands. "Nice and solid," she said, in the same voice I'd heard her use in some of L.A.'s finer restaurants. I almost expected her to keep on—*full-bodied, with just a hint of mischief*—and was a little disappointed when she didn't. "Any warranties?" she asked, ever practical.

"Two weeks," the kid said, and I pictured a gaggle of women rushing back to their bedrooms so they'd be sure to get their money's worth before the contraption died.

"Just two?" I asked.

"After that, the regular manufacturer's warranty

kicks in for a year," he said, apparently not noticing my irony.

Carla turned the thing this way and that, almost as if it were a mango and she were looking for bruises. "Japanese?"

He nodded, all smiles, happy to be selling to a connoisseur. "A fabulous model." He took it back from her, then proceeded to bend the pink shaft into a decidedly unnatural position. He flipped the switch and the whole thing turned into a rather obscene whirligig. "You can get amazing control this way." He looked straight at me, as if he could tell I was the detractor. "Maximum penetration."

I tried to swallow, managed a cough, and was certain my cheeks were going to set off the sprinkler system.

"How about it?" Carla asked.

I wrinkled my nose. "I don't think so."

"Oh, come on, Mattie. That's why we're here, remember?"

This time, I turned my back to the counter and lowered my voice. "No bear is going fishing near my…" I twirled my hand loosely in the air.

"We have a nice model with a beaver," the kid said.

Reluctantly, I turned around, letting him back into the conversation. "That's even worse," I said, wondering about the sense of humor necessary to invent a vibrator buttressed with a beaver.

"I never knew you were such a prude. So much for the mystery behind that eighteen percent."

I scowled at Carla and turned to the clerk. "Got anything else?"

"The Love Bunny's very popular." He pulled it out and plunked it on the counter. A nice soft shade of pink and a sweet little long-eared bunny rabbit.

Aw, shucks, how cute is that?

I wanted to be cynical, really I did. But I had to admit, the Bunny was truly adorable. And, in truth, I wanted to own one of these gizmos. They seemed…*intriguing,* and I wanted to take one home for a test drive. After all, with just one thin wall separating me and Cullen Slater…

I stifled a little shiver as my thighs began to melt.

The simple fact was, it might take me a while to work up the nerve to talk to Slater. But in the meantime, surely I could work up the nerve to rev up the Love Bunny. Right?

Right.

"Oh, wow." Carla's hoarse whisper pulled me away from my Cullen fantasy. She'd moved to the far end of the case, and was looking at something just around the corner and fanning herself with one of the store's postcards.

Knowing I'd regret it, I circled the case, wanting to see for myself what had struck such a note of awe into Carla's usually calm and collected voice.

Oh, wow was right.

"Maybe you should get a dildo," Carla said.

"Those can't possibly be anatomically correct," I said.

But they were, the kid assured us. And human, too. The incredibly large, incredibly lifelike dildos filling the glass case were, in fact, exact replicas of the very real, very lucrative packages of some porn stars I'd never heard of before.

"Just how exact?" Carla asked.

"Exact," the kid said.

I imagined a roomful of guys walking around with plastered penises, sacrificing their dignity for the pleasure of women—and gay men—everywhere.

"Should we?" Carla asked. She held up a condom package. "You need the practice, and Cullen might be…"

The thought that Cullen could give a horse a run for his money was both exciting and terrifying. But no. I still had a few lines in the sand, and monster dildos were on the far, far, far side of that line. "I think just the Bunny."

"Good choice," the kid said.

Carla shrugged. "Whatever." She headed toward the back of the store, then turned around to make sure I was following. I wasn't. "Are you coming?"

"Aren't we done?"

"Don't be silly." She nodded toward the box on the counter. "That's just the little black dress. We still have to buy you some accessories."

I glanced from the door to Carla, then back to the door. What the hell. I was already here, and I did have a plan. And if I wanted some experience—and I *did* want experience—I was probably going to need the sex toy equivalent of pearls, a beaded handbag and strappy sandals.

Mostly in black leather, I presumed.

5

THE PLEASURE PALACE
Thanks for shopping with us

Love Bunny, model A (warr.) $95.99

Venus Glide lubricant (raspberry) $8.95

Eros Condom Assortment Box (4 doz.) $30.00

Fur-lined mask $14.95

Leather halter, blk $59.95

Fancy Pants crotchless panties $15.50

(2) Penis Pasta $20.50

Blue Balls, penis-shaped ice cube tray $8.95

Sensuality Candles (set of 2) $17.75

Maid-2-Order teddy/panty set $59.95

Penis illuminated holiday ornaments $19.95

He's So Hot candles (set of 2) $10.50

Bound-2-U wrist restraints $19.95

Sub-Total **$382.89**

Sales Tax $31.59

Total **$414.48**

Tendered by Credit Card $414.48

Balance Due . . . . $ 00.00

Satisfaction guaranteed or your money back!

THREE HOURS AND OVER FOUR hundred dollars later, Carla and I headed toward my apartment, laden with plain, brown paper bags stuffed full of the basic necessities of slutdom, along with a few extra novelties to spice up my first annual slut-o-rama party. Pragmatic to the end, Carla had decided that if I lacked some basic skills, probably a lot of my friends did, too. So while Carla maneuvered us through the San Fernando Valley toward Studio City, I started burning up the cellular airwaves.

By the time she'd managed to parallel park in front of my building, I had firm commitments for the next night from two girlfriends and Greg Martin. If nothing else, I figured Greg could provide a valuable insight into the whole condom quandary.

"I figure we'll use the penis pasta for a light salad, don't you think?"

We were heading up the stairs as I stifled a giggle, wondering if I could actually eat a penis pasta salad without choking.

"And we'll serve drinks like sex on the beach and screaming orgasms," she continued. "It'll be a blast."

My stomach was already starting to ache from holding back laughter. "So when everyone's had a few orgasms, that's when we whip out the Love Bunny. Seems backward, somehow."

"True." Carla stopped in front of my door and turned to face me, her mouth twitching. She shifted a bag, and pulled her key chain out of her pocket. "Oh, damn. I don't have your key on me."

"I've got it." I half leaned against the railing, balancing the bigger bag on my hip, then dug around inside my purse until I found my keys. The second I tossed them to her, the door behind her opened, and Cullen Slater sauntered out—lean and luscious as always.

I swallowed a gasp and willed my eyes not to veer toward the part of his anatomy I already had on the brain.

But when his eyes met mine, all my good intentions went to hell in a hand-basket. I glanced down toward it, swallowed again, and ripped my gaze away. I was certain he knew exactly where I'd been looking. From his smile, I wasn't sure he cared.

"Hey, Mattie," he said, his voice just as sexy as his body. "Any chance I can come in? Pick up my mail?"

"I…um…sure," I squeaked, the idea of Cullen coming anywhere throwing me completely for a loop.

At the same time, the door across the hall opened. Or, more accurately, the door across the walkway opened, since the hall is technically a balcony. All our apartments open to the outside, with the complex forming a rectangle, the center of which is taken up primarily by the pool.

I immediately looked toward the sound of the door, and saw Mike stepping from his apartment. He looked at me, looked at Cullen, then looked back at me. Then he smiled. And not just any smile. No, this smile suggested that he knew exactly what I was up to.

Completely unsettled—and at the same time certain I was imagining things—I took an involuntary step forward, stumbled over my own feet, and managed to drop both of my bags. They tumbled out of my hands, and the contents—and condoms—went flying, a few of the sample condoms the clerk had thrown in as a bonus actually rolling off the balcony and dropping to the pool deck below.

Great.

An extra large superlubed version in bright pink foil shot past Cullen just as a blond bombshell stepped out of his apartment. It landed right in front of her strappy Emanuel Ungaro sandal. She shot me a withering look, pushed the thing away with her toe, and latched onto Cullen's arm.

Carla lost it, leaning in to bury her face against my door as she shook with silent laughter. I heard a chortle from Mike's direction, too, but couldn't bring myself to look that way.

I considered dying on the spot, but fate wasn't co-operating.

Instead, I got down on my hands and knees and started to gather my toys. One box of penis pasta had broken open, and now the walkway was littered with tiny male privates. I managed to scoop up a handful and dumped them into my bag.

Cullen took a step toward me, then bent down, his thighs straining against the worn denim. He reached behind a planter and picked up the Love Bunny's box. "I think this belongs to you," he said, his gorgeous face completely unreadable. "And I'll just get my mail later."

I nodded, mute, as my fingers closed around the box. It occurred to me that I'd crossed some sort of cosmic marker. Embarrassment was no longer possible. Instead, I planted my rump on the concrete, and laughed until I was sure I'd burst an internal organ.

Slater's perfect date stepped over me, careful not to come too close, probably for fear my disease was catching. Slater followed, and I managed to choke back a guffaw long enough to look up. For just a second, I thought I saw a sliver of amusement dance across his oh-so-stoic face. But then he turned, took Miss Perfect's elbow, and headed down the stairs—passing my sister Angie in the process.

Huh?

I did a double take, because Angie was supposed to be tucked away in her downtown office or lounging by the pool behind her Beverly Hills bungalow. She never deigned to come to the valley, always forcing me to go to the west side for lunch or whatever. So, naturally, she picked today to break her steadfast rule, simply so that she could catch me at full embarrassment potential.

Great.

Actually, Angie was the least of it. Everywhere I turned, I saw witnesses to my humiliation. Cullen, Mike, Angie, the blond bimbo. Honestly, it was all to much.

And all I could do was sit there, gazing wistfully in the direction that Cullen had disappeared, and hope that I hadn't completely blown my chances. With Cullen, or with the television show.

Or, a mischievous little voice said in my head, *with Mike.*

AFTER CULLEN AND BIMBO-BABE disappeared, Mike moved in and helped me, Angie and Carla clean up the mess. He said nothing about the content of the bags, and I have to admit I admired his restraint.

When everything was packed up, he headed back

to his apartment, paused in his doorway, and said, "See you at seven."

I nodded, mute, sure that my cheeks were burning. Then I escaped into my own apartment, my sister and best friend trailing behind me.

"Seven?" Carla said, as soon as the door closed behind us. "What happens at seven?"

I waved my hand, signaling a nonevent. "Nothing. He helped me put together that thing," I said, pointing to my new filing cabinet. "So I returned the favor by promising to help him hang shelves."

"Uh-huh," Angie said, her tone dubious.

"Give it up, Mat," Carla said. "You're going over there because he's hot."

I lifted my eyebrows and tried to look put-upon. "I *so* am not! In case you've already forgotten, we laid out the entire path of my love life not two hours ago. And Mike Peterson was not part of it."

"Not part of your *sex* life," Carla clarified. "We didn't talk about your love life at all."

"Well, if I'm going to be boinking Cullen, I'm certainly not going to be having a love life with Mike."

"*There!* See?" Carla pointed at me triumphantly. "You're already thinking in terms of love with him."

"No, I am not," I said, even though a rebellious

little bit of my mind had entertained the idea. "And what is with you, anyway? You're the one who insisted that me going after Cullen would make Emmy-winning television."

"Whoa there!" Angie had been watching us like you might watch a tennis game, but now she held up a hand. "In love with Mike? Boinking Cullen on television?"

"Not *on* television," I said. *"Ewww!"*

Angie gave me one of her looks. "I'm not interested in semantics. I'm interested in what you're up to."

I caught Carla's eye, and she shrugged. Since I knew better than to try to keep a secret from Angie, I laid everything out for her. My crappy eighteen percent. My plan to enlist Cullen's services to up that score. My subsequent hesitation based on the fact that the plan was utter lunacy. And finally Carla's television scheme, which considerably upped my interest in the whole bedding-Cullen plan.

"But you're not interested in actually dating the guy?" Angie asked.

I shook my head. "Long-term, I seriously don't think he's my type."

"But for a wild fling," Carla put in, "he's perfect."

Angie's lips curved up. "He is rather hot, isn't

he?" Before I could answer, she fired a question at me. "But Mike isn't perfect? Why not?"

"Mike's hardly ratings-worthy," said Carla.

I aimed a scowl in her direction. "That's not it at all," I said. "Mike's your typical, basic, all-around nice guy. And I've done that already. With Dex. It was a nightmare. A personal, never-to-be-repeated nightmare. I need..." I trailed off, shrugging.

"A fling," Angie said. "Wild, hot sex. Yeah, I get that."

I squinted at her. "You do?"

"Absolutely." A sly grin slid across her mouth. "Not that *I* need a fling. I got eighty-five percent on that test."

"No kidding?" Carla asked, clearly impressed. Angie just breathed on her nails and pretended to buff them on her shirtfront, basking in yet another victory over her sister. *Moi.*

"So you understand?"

"I totally understand," my sister said. "You're doing what you have to do—and using this guy Cullen—to get what you want. Hot sex and a television gig. Sounds damn reasonable of you, really."

Actually, put that way, it sounded cold and calculating, but I tried not to think about that. I *did* have a plan, and it was a good one. And in light of what I knew about Cullen and his revolving door bedroom, I honestly don't think he'd mind too much playing stud of the week.

"Listen," Angie continued. "What you do is your business. I'm not here to criticize your completely whacked plans."

"That makes me feel so much better," I said dryly. "What exactly *are* you here for?"

"I'm having my walls painted and the carpet replaced with hardwood. The fumes were just too much, so I thought I'd come crash with my darling sister."

"Uh-huh." As I've already mentioned, Angie doesn't do the San Fernando Valley. So I wasn't buying this.

She lifted a shoulder. "Okay, I'm not actually crashing here the whole time. I'm staying at the Four Seasons."

I held back a sarcastic remark. My sister—an investment banker—is just the kind who would stay at a luxury hotel during a remodel. Angie hadn't veered off the family-ordained path at all. Which meant that in my parents' eyes, she was clearly the favored child. The winner. The best.

Honestly, it drove me a little crazy.

"For the next couple of days, though, I'm

sleeping here." I blinked at that. Angie? Deigning to sleep on a couch?

"Why?"

"Some conference at the hotel. I couldn't get a suite."

"Ah. So you'd rather sleep on my couch."

She looped an arm around my shoulder. "You're my darling little sister," she said with an evil gleam in her eyes.

I laughed and elbowed her in the ribs. "By three months."

"Chronologically, maybe. Maturation-wise, I'd say I'm years ahead of you."

Since this kind of bickering could last for hours, I just nodded. "Fine," I said, thinking of all my privacy that had just been shot to hell. Not that I did much that really needed privacy; it was just the principle of the thing.

"Don't worry about helping me," she said. "I've only got one bag." She headed for the door and paused, but I took her at her word and didn't offer to help. Bitchy, maybe, but I wanted to talk with Carla.

"She's going to totally screw this up," I said, the second the door closed behind my sister.

"How?" Carla said. "Angie's just Angie. And, yes, she's a little brash, but that comes from living with your parents. I mean, look at how screwed up you are."

I ignored that part and focused on my real concern, enunciating so that she'd understand how serious I was. "Angie is never *just* Angie. And if I'm going after the hot male model, you can be certain *she's* going to go after him, too."

"Don't be silly," Carla said. "She wouldn't do tha—" She cut herself off midsentence. "Actually, you're right. This is Angie we're talking about. She totally would."

"Yup." I love my sister, but she's highly competitive. This is not necessarily a bad thing. Part of the reason I did so well in school, I'm sure, is that I desperately wanted to stay one step ahead of Angie. If she'd been a C-student, that wouldn't have been hard. But she's smart and competitive, and wanted that valedictorian plaque as much as I did.

Too bad for me, she ended up getting it. And I had to smile and say congratulations and pretend like I didn't want to smack her.

That urge had been especially hard to suppress since I'd actually had a shot in academia. Where men were concerned, Angie had always had me beat by a very wide margin.

At any rate, the point is that Angie has the wherewithal to be serious competition for me in the men department. And if she wanted to throw a monkey wrench into my whole convoluted Cullen plan…well, I'd be hard pressed to stop her.

Carla, of course, already knew all that; I'd cried on her shoulder plenty in junior high and high school. Even so, I laid it all out for her again.

"Well," she said, once I was done spilling my insecure little guts. "Even if she does try to horn in on the Cullen action, it won't be a disaster."

"Are you kidding? It would be a total disaster!"

"Ratings," Carla said. "Viewers love catfights. And a catfight between sisters…"

She didn't bother finishing the thought. There was no need; I could see where she was going just fine. I worked in reality television, after all. Catfights. Sibling rivalry. Bizarre family dysfunctions. It was all there, sucking in the ratings. Carla was right. If there was a battle between me and Angie for Cullen's affections (for lack of a better word), the end result could only be more zing for my screenplay.

For about three seconds, I felt a deep shame for my chosen profession. Then I remembered that writing this script *wasn't* my chosen career. It was a stepping stone. And so long as I stepped carefully, I'd be just fine.

Besides, I knew there was no way in hell that I'd back away, not now that I had an actual plan to reach my goal. I *would* be a screenwriter. I was willing to go to the wire if that's what it took because I wanted it so much. *Needed* it so much.

The desire burned a hole through my gut, but I trusted it. Nothing about my writing stemmed from a desire to compete, with Angie or anyone else. It was purely me. And no matter what I had to do—work at bad reality-show production companies or seduce hunky neighbors—I knew that I would someday be a screenwriter.

Fortunately, this entire thought process didn't take too long, so I was back on track with my plan—despite my uninvited sister—when said sister returned with her suitcase.

"You guys have fun," Carla said, wiggling her fingers as she headed for the door, basically, abandoning me.

"Right," I said, shutting the door after Carla and turning to my sister. "So, just toss your stuff anywhere."

She did, dumping her bag next to the couch. Even though it was only three, we opened a bottle of red wine, kicked back and spent the afternoon playing catch-up.

I was uncorking our third bottle of wine, when I glanced at the clock. "Shit!" I stood up, almost spilling the wine and managing to dump over the bowl of tortilla chips I'd centered between us on the couch.

"What?"

"I forgot about Mike. I told him I'd help him hang shelves tonight. I'm already five minutes late!"

"Well, let's go." She stood up, too, then took a step for the door, her wineglass still firmly in hand.

"*Let's* go?" I just stood there, staring at her.

"Sure. Why not?"

"Well, I…because…" I trailed off, because what could I say? That some little something inside of me wanted alone-time with Mike? How ridiculous was that? He was just a nice guy in the building.

The corner of Angie's lip curled up, as if she knew exactly what I was thinking. "Come on, Mat," she said. "I mean, this isn't a date, right? It's not as if I would be intruding, would it?"

"Of course not. But—"

"And if you're helping him hang shelves, an extra hand will come in handy." She took a step toward the door. "Come on. We're late."

And since there was no reasonable or rationale way for me to argue, I followed, my emotions all in a muddle. Two hours ago, I'd been annoyed at the possibility that my sister might try to interfere with Cullen and mess up my chances with the show. Okay, fair enough. But that was all about the show. It wasn't personal. And I could deal with it. Angie and I had been competing our whole lives; this wasn't exactly new territory.

But with Mike, something had shifted. Her wanting to head over to his place. Saying he was cute. Offering to help hang his shelves…

I don't know. Nothing about that was overtly competitive. Or even remotely suggested that she had any interest in the guy.

But to me…well, to me it felt completely personal. And *that* is what freaked me out. Because I shouldn't care about her getting personal with Mike. He was on my list as a friend, and only a friend.

The thing is, I think the list in my head wasn't quite in synch with the rest of my emotions.

And, that scared the hell out of me.

MIKE KNEW HE WAS IN trouble. Big trouble. Because he was head over heels, totally in lust with Mattie Brown.

He'd known it, of course, from the first moment he'd seen her. His interest—and determination—had been piqued when he'd overheard her plan to ratchet up her sex drive. And he'd been absolutely certain of the extent to which he'd fallen when he'd realized that her efforts were aimed at Cullen Slater.

Mike had never been the kind of guy to question his own looks or to feel uncomfortable around other men. But he had to admit that Cullen—he of the male model photo shoot and supermodel overnight guests—was stiff competition. And the idea of Mattie hooking up with Cullen made Mike's blood boil. So much so that he'd had to restrain himself from saying something after she'd spilled her Pleasure Palace loot all over the balcony.

And it wasn't just words he'd had to restrain himself from. His instinct had been to ignore the mess and gather her in his arms. To wipe away the mortification he'd seen on her face and to cover her with kisses.

Damn, but he was far gone. All Mattie had to do was say, "Jump," and Mike would ask, "How high?"

Bottom line? He knew he had it bad. But he hadn't really known just *how* bad until he'd been knocked sideways by the punch-in-the-gut feeling that had assaulted him when she'd shown up at his door with her sister in tow. He'd wanted her all alone, all to himself. And it had taken all his self-control to be nice to Angie in those first few minutes.

To give himself credit, his good manners had returned quickly, and he'd even enjoyed Angie's company. She seemed nice enough and—unless he was completely off base—she even knew that he had the hots for Mattie. Not that Angie actually said anything. It was more the little things she did. The way she watched him watching Mattie. The way she'd shifted sideways so that he was standing next to Mattie as he measured for his newly bought shelves. The way she'd moved to the chair so that the only place for him to sit once they'd started *The Thin Man* was on the couch, right next to her sister.

Considering all that, he had to say he liked the woman. For that matter, he wondered if maybe she could be an ally in his fight to position himself above Cullen in the hierarchy of Mattie's plan. Not that he knew how to broach the subject with Angie. But the whole Mattie-Cullen-sexpertise dilemma kept bouncing through his head, so much that he realized he wasn't paying a bit of attention to the movie. Or to anything else, for that matter.

Which would explain why he was so surprised when the room suddenly became silent and the image on his television screen froze. He turned, looking over to Mattie who'd been sitting beside him, as immersed in the movie as he was in his own thoughts.

"Sorry," she said. "Can I use your bathroom?"

"Of course." He stood up when she did, feeling overly chivalrous, and covered the movement by heading to the kitchen. Angie followed him.

"Thanks for putting up with me," she said. "I

know you were only expecting to serve pizza and wine to one."

"Oh, no problem," he said, grabbing a corkscrew just so he'd have something to do with his hands. He focused on the bottle, looking up only when he heard her snicker. "You don't believe me?"

She shook her head. "Not at all."

The statement wasn't accusatory, and he relaxed, sensing an ally. "What then?"

"I just think that you and my sister would make a cute couple."

"Do you?" He turned back to the wine bottle, focusing intently so that she couldn't see his face. "Interesting perspective considering you only arrived on the scene a few hours ago."

"You can learn a lot in a few hours," she said. "See a lot, too."

"Perhaps you've seen that your sister has a bit of a thing for her next-door neighbor."

"You're her neighbor."

"I'm across the hall," he said. "That can make all the difference."

"Mmm." She moved into the kitchen, sidling behind him to open the fridge and grab a soda. Which left him with the untenable choice of turning to talk to her or being rude and keeping his back to her. His momma, however, didn't raise a boy with no manners. He turned. And she smiled. "Just between you and me, all that nonsense between her and Cullen is just for show." She rolled her eyes. "Literally, for show."

Mike wanted to ask her what she meant, but he didn't have the chance because he heard the bathroom door creak open and Mattie's approaching footsteps. Seconds later, Mattie appeared around the corner. "Hey," she said. "Snack break?"

"Just saying goodbye," Angie said, lifting her glass in a toast. "To Nick and Nora. You two enjoy the rest of their movie."

"But—"

Angie cut her sister off with a wave. "Honestly, Mat, I'm exhausted. I spent the day dealing with contractors. I can feel the migraine creeping up my spine."

"Oh." Mattie looked at him, and for a tiny second, he let himself believe that he saw a hint of pleasure in her eyes. "Oh, well, if you need me to go back with you…"

"No, no, no," Angie said, waving a hand that Mike wanted to kiss in gratitude. "You watch the end of the flick. I'm just going to go crash."

"Great. Right. The movie. Yes." She reached out and grabbed the glass that Mike had refilled. "And wine. Definitely want more wine." And then she turned and headed into the living room.

"You're on your own," Angie whispered, low enough so that only Mike heard. "Go for it."

And as he gaped after her, Angie turned and left, leaving him standing like an idiot in the kitchen wondering what to do next. Wondering, more, what Angie had meant when she'd said the Cullen thing was all for show. And wondering most of all how bold he was willing to be with the woman who was, right at that very moment, drinking wine on his couch.

Since the various diplomas on Mike's office wall proved he wasn't a stupid man, it didn't take long for him to arrive at one inescapable conclusion. The time to go for it was now. The only question was how.

He was still considering that question when he went back into the living area. Mattie smiled up at him and patted the couch even as she aimed the remote at the television. "Ready to finish the film?"

"Absolutely," he said, sitting beside her, just a little bit closer than ordinary rules of personal space allowed. She didn't slide away, though. In fact, she even leaned closer, and Mike held his breath, his heart beating fast, as she reached across him for the roll of paper towels he'd tossed onto the coffee table for them to use as napkins.

He didn't manage to concentrate on the remainder of the movie any more than he had on the beginning. But he had a feeling that Mattie's concentration was divided, too. Every time he looked in her direction, he caught her glancing in his. The whole situation reeked of high school, making his hands sweat and his cock hard. But it was the best part of high school. That first date attraction, when you just knew that she liked you, too, but weren't quite sure how to take it to the next level.

Fortunately for Mike, he wasn't still in high school; he *did* know how to move past the glorious high of attraction and into the even greater rewards of the bedroom.

All that remained was to actually do it.

As soon as the credits started to roll, Mattie leaned back and sighed deeply. "I love that movie."

"So do I," Mike said, looking at her and not the screen.

"What's your favorite part?"

"Ah," he said, wishing he'd actually watched the movie earlier in the afternoon like he'd planned. "I'm, uh, actually pretty fond of the dog."

"Asta? Me, too. For years I wanted a dog just like him. Too bad I'm allergic."

"I had a Lab growing up," he said, hoping they

could veer away from the dangerous subject of the film in question. "A boy and his dog. You know. Typical childhood."

"Mine wasn't typical at all. I'm such a geek. All I did was study and watch movies and listen to soundtracks. Very antisocial." She stood up and moved to the television stand, where he'd left the DVD case. "I can't believe I don't already own this. I just love this series." She smiled up at him, her eyes dancing. "I don't suppose you have all of them?"

"Ah, no," he said, fighting the urge to tell yet another lie to lure her into his living room.

"Too bad. I adore Jimmy Stewart."

"William Powell," he said, proud of himself for catching her in a mistake. "He's the thin man." At the very least that should solidify his claim that he knew something about this series of films.

From the way she was squinting at him, though, he had to wonder if he hadn't just made the verbal equivalent of stepping in a pile of shit.

"William Powell is Nick Charles," she said. "The thin man is the body they find. And one of Jimmy Stewart's very early roles was in *After the Thin Man*."

"Right," he said. "Sure."

She crossed her arms over her chest, and Mike was relieved to see that she didn't look irritated, just a little baffled. And maybe a lot amused. "I thought you loved this series."

"Theoretically, I do," he said.

That actually earned him a laugh. "Uh-huh," she said, her expression stern but her tone laced with restrained laughter. "And, um, just how theoretical is that passion?"

"Let's just say that if I knew anything at all about the series, I'm sure I'd be enthralled."

She pressed her lips tight together, then looked down at the carpet, her shoulders shaking with laughter. "I have no idea why I'm laughing," she finally said. "I have a feeling I'm supposed to be annoyed with you. It's got to be the wine."

"Definitely the alcohol," he agreed. "All part of my master plan. And at the risk of digging myself in deeper, before you decide you're annoyed and leave, could you explain to me why the whole series of movies refers to *The Thin Man* if the poor guy is dead?"

At that, she burst out into genuine laughter and sank onto his couch. He sank down beside her.

"I can't," she said, patting his knee, the touch alone sending his body reeling. "It's one of those unsolvable Hollywood mysteries."

"Damn," he said. "And I thought I'd caught myself an expert."

"Which raises an interesting question," she said, turning to him. "Why exactly did you tell me you loved the movie? For that matter, why do you *own* the movie?" Then her eyes widened and her mouth formed a little O. "Wait a sec. You bought it today."

"Also guilty," he said. "And, really, do you need to ask?"

He was watching her eyes, keeping his gaze fixed on hers, silently daring her to look away. Her gaze never wavered, but she did nod. Just a tiny lift of her chin, then a single, soft, "Yes. I need to ask."

"Age-old story," he said, watching her face carefully. "You're my first friend in the building. I was looking for a connection. You know."

"Friend," she said. "Right."

Inside, Mike's heart was doing flip-flops. Because even though her voice was steady, her eyes and her hands weren't. There was a hint of disappointment shining through her manner. And in that split second, he knew that Angie had been right. There was a connection between them. A connection that he fully intended to strengthen. Right then, right there.

She cleared her throat. "Right," she said again. "So, um, what did you think of the movie?"

"I don't know," he said honestly. "I can't say that I've ever really seen it."

Her teeth played softly over her lower lip, and her eyes cut to the television. "We just sat here for two hours and watched it."

"I didn't," he said. And then he reached over and took a loose strand of her hair, letting it flow over his fingers, crackling with the electricity that seemed to arc between them.

"You didn't?" she said, her voice so soft he could barely hear her.

"No," he said. "I was watching you."

6

"ME?" MY VOICE sounded high, like somebody else's. Which I think was appropriate because I felt like someone else. Or, more accurately, I felt like someone in a dream. "Why were you watching me?"

I asked the question only so that I would have something to say. Because I knew that if I didn't say anything, he would have to kiss me. And I *wanted* him to kiss me. Wanted it desperately, in fact.

But what if he *didn't* kiss me?

Oh, dear Lord, this was why I was so pathetic with men.

The thought skittered through my head, bringing with it a flurry of nerves. Of course, I overcompensated by talking more. "Mike. Why were you watching me?"

He brushed his fingertip over my lower lip, the contact both daring and a little bit hesitant. There was nothing hesitant about my reaction, though. Sparks shot though me, converging in hot points at my nipples and between my thighs. I think I moaned a little and, thank God, that was all the encouragement Mike needed.

He leaned closer, the touch of his lips replacing the touch of his finger, and sending spirals of passion screaming through my soul. Some tiny part of my head was screaming for me to stop, that this wasn't what I wanted. That I had a *plan*, dammit!

But the rest of me was ignoring that annoyingly loud voice in my head. Because the rest of me was falling into a pile of warm goo. The kind that I wanted to lose myself in as much as I wanted to lose myself in Mike's touch.

And then, suddenly, the warmth of his lips was gone. I opened my eyes, staring accusatorily at him. "Wha—"

He silenced me with a gentle finger. "I want you, Mattie. But if you don't want to stay…"

He trailed off, leaving a gaping question between us and—damn him—making the decision entirely mine.

I knew what I *should* do, of course. I should walk away. Mike wasn't the man I was after. Not for the long term and not even for a fling.

Except I wasn't walking. For better or for worse,

I was staying right there. Even more, I was boldly leaning forward to slide my fingers through his hair. And, yes, to press my mouth against his.

MIKE WANTED TO PINCH HIMSELF, because he was certain this couldn't be real. This had to be a dream. Like the dreams he'd been having every night since he'd first met Mattie. The dream where she came into his arms, pressed soft kisses to his lips, and begged for him to make love to her.

But this wasn't a dream, and no pinches were necessary. This was real. The lips that his brushed belonged to Mattie. Her heady scent—like soap and strawberries—filled his senses. And so help him, he wanted to stand on the couch and beat his chest like Tarzan, claiming victory. Proclaiming himself the king of the world.

Instead, he pulled his lips away from hers only long enough to utter the only soft sound that he could manage. "Mattie."

She moaned in response, then cleaved to him again, her need as desperate as his own. "Don't talk," she whispered. "Don't make me think about this."

He wanted to nod, wanted to tell her that if there was any thinking to be done that he could manage for the both of them. Except, apparently he couldn't.

His thoughts were in a muddle, replaced with primal images. Her lips. Her neck. Her breast.

One by one, he followed the path of those thoughts. His mouth first concentrating on her lips, even as his hands roamed the rest of her body, exploring curves and slipping under clothing to find the soft skin below.

He stroked her back, and she sighed deeply, the sound even more intense when he slid his hands up, his fingers splayed, and his thumbs reaching to her front to brush the soft skin near her breasts.

Her hands pressed against his chest, her palms open against him, her skin separated from his by nothing more than the thin layer of his T-shirt. The heat from her hands filled him, shot through him, and made him even harder. But as astounding as it might sound, his own body was almost extraneous to him at the moment. All he wanted was to touch her. To please her. To see her body writhe against his and her hear soft moans.

He wanted to make her come. Hell, he wanted to watch her come.

She shifted in his embrace, forcing his hand to move from her back around her side until his palm cupped her breast. Her nipple was like a hard nub, and he couldn't help himself. He had to taste it.

He bent down, taking her breast in his mouth even through her blouse. She wasn't wearing a bra, but even so, the interference between skin on skin was too frustrating. Too cloying.

"Take it off," she said, removing her hands from his chest so that she could go to work on her buttons.

He helped her along, or tried to. After a few fumbling attempts he still didn't have the shirt off her. "Just rip the damn thing off," she said.

"You're sure?"

"Mike..."

His heart flip-flopped. And since there was no way he was arguing with a woman whose voice carried that much desperation, he did as she asked. He ripped, pulling the shirt open from the middle. Buttons flew, and he peeled it back, exposing her breasts and trapping her arms at her sides. He made a little sound, like a blind man suddenly cured seeing a sunset for the first time. And then he buried himself against her, his cheek stroking her breast before he turned to capture her with his mouth.

He played his tongue over her nipple, delighting in the way she squirmed under him, seeking a release that he wasn't yet ready to give her. Soon, yes. But not quite yet. Not until he could see in her eyes that she truly couldn't take any more.

He slid his hand down, stroking the soft skin of her stomach, letting his fingers dance over the buckle of her belt. He released it handily, loosening the waistband of her low-slung jeans in the process. One more flick of the button and a quick tug on her fly, and his fingers were that much closer to heaven.

Her panties were silk, soft and warm, and he let his fingers glide down in a warm, sensuous motion. She bucked softly, encouraging him, her excited response making him that much harder. Her hips lifted, and he took the opportunity to slide his hand down, cupping her sex, then sliding his finger under the crotch of her panties to find a treasure trove of wet velvet.

He groaned, his entire body aflame, and as his finger slid inside her, he pressed kisses roughly up her body, finally meeting her lips. She opened to him eagerly, as if she'd been holding her breath through his explorations, just waiting for his lips to find hers so that she could taste him and consume him.

Their kisses deepened, the thrust of their tongues matching the thrust of his finger. Her hips arched and bucked, and when she softly pleaded with him as her fingers reached for his own zipper, he knew that he couldn't wait any longer.

"Mattie," he whispered, forcing the word out

past a wall of longing. He leaned back, hating the space that grew between them as he pulled his T-shirt over his head.

Her eyes went wide, and he saw a smile dance on her lips as he shimmied out of his jeans. "About time," she said.

"Good things come to those who wait," he countered.

"So I see." She reached out, stroking his erection through the cotton of his boxers. "Yes, very good."

Her voice was laced with a tease that he was more than willing to return. "Not good," he said. "Excellent. But don't grade me yet. Wait until you take a test drive."

"Is that what we're doing?" she asked, kicking her own jeans off. She knelt on the floor, her bare legs on a flannel blanket that had slid off the couch only moments before.

"Oh, yeah," he said, watching as she extricated herself from her shirt. He moved closer, and his hands closed over the waistband of her panties. He bent forward, kissing her breasts, then drawing a line down to her belly button with his lips. Lower and lower and lower still until he found her sweet center.

She laid back, resting her head on a battered sofa cushion as she moved rhythmically under him, making soft noises that drove him on, exciting him and making him wonder how he'd ever survived without the sound of her, the feel of her. The taste of her.

He brought her to the edge, then slid up her body, their slick skin sliding together as if made for each other. He kissed her, soft and gentle, but she wasn't having any of that. Her fingernails dug into his shoulder blades. "Now," she said. "Don't you dare stop."

Never one to disappoint, Mike stopped only long enough to slip on a condom, then thrust inside her, his fingers teasing her clit as he moved, rhythmically losing himself to heaven, and coming closer and closer until, finally, the explosion in her body drove him over the edge. His body shattered, came back together and then, when he thought he just might die from the pleasure of it, he fell, exhausted, beside her, the floor hard and unyielding beneath them. She sighed happily and shifted a little, rubbing her rear against his cock.

"That's all?" she asked, a tease in her voice.

"Give a guy a second to recharge."

"One one-thousand…two one-thousand…"

He leaned closer and nipped her shoulder with his teeth. She giggled and squirmed in his arms, ending up facing him, her eyes bright even in the dim light of the room.

"Hey," she whispered, then scooted lower, finally pressing her head against his chest. "This is nice."

He stroked her hair, his fingers combing the long, smooth strands. "Very nice," he said. Very, very, *very* nice.

A warm flood of emotion spread through him. Not hard and urgent as it had been earlier, when he'd been certain that he'd die if he didn't come inside her right then, but soft and gentle. *Contentment,* he realized.

This was what he'd wanted for days, and tonight he'd taken a risk to go after what he wanted. It had paid off, too, he thought, looking at her forehead, the curve of her ear, and her softly parted lips.

She'd come willingly, even eagerly into his arms. Her body had responded to his as if they'd been made for each other. And his heart…well, his heart had found its mate.

He let his fingers trace idly over her body, watching the way she squirmed under his touch even as he tried to discern what was in her heart. Had she lost herself, too? Or was she merely biding time to her next encounter? Her next man? A typical date in the wilds of Los Angeles?

He couldn't bear the thought. Even more, he couldn't stomach the idea of the man she might go to next. He'd found his own personal heaven in this woman's arms, and he'd be damned if he'd lose her. Not to Cullen Slater. Not to anyone.

Wow.

I mean, can I just say... *Wow.*

And then, because I thought he ought to hear it, too, I turned toward Mike, kissed his ear, and said, "Wow."

He laughed. "Sweetheart, you haven't seen anything. That was just the appetizer."

I pretended to groan, then leaned back onto our blanket. "If that's only the first course, then let me state for the record that I intend to become a gourmand. Maybe even a glutton. And I *definitely* intend to thoroughly savor all the courses."

"Ah, well, zee chef, he eez flattered. Zee chef wonders if five courses will satisfy a palate as discerning as zee lady's."

I laughed. "Oh, yeah. I think I can handle that." At the moment, frankly, I was up for pretty much anything. True, we hadn't had the kind of sex that was going to do much for my slut score, but it sure did a lot for my ego. I felt beautiful and cherished and thoroughly sated. And believe me, that was a very heady combination.

At the same time, some little part of me knew that this whole situation was ripe for disaster. I needed to leave. To pull myself together. To focus on my career. That one thing I'd supposedly been single-mindedly aiming for my entire life.

But I figured my career wasn't going to be taking off in the next few hours. The future would come soon enough and I'd have to walk out Mike's door. In the meantime, I just wanted him to hold me. And, you know, make love to me. At least four more times...

With a delighted laugh, I rolled over, then strad-dled him and planted a kiss on his delicious lips. I felt his body rise to attention, and I wiggled my rear a little, trying to urge him along.

"Hey," he said.

"Hey yourself." I shifted again, running my hands over his chest, feeling a feminine power rise within me as I saw the delighted gleam in his eye. I bent down and nipped at his lower lip. He reached down and stroked between my legs. And all of a sudden, playtime was over. I wanted serious touches, and I wanted them now.

"I'm ready for the next course," I whispered, unable to keep my hands from running all over his smooth skin.

"Baby," Mike said as he leaned up to kiss me, "I thought you'd never ask."

THE SECOND I WOKE UP, I *knew* that I should have left hours ago. It was already after seven, the morning sun was streaming in through the windows, and I was feeling like an idiot. A thoroughly limp, extremely satisfied idiot.

At some point in the night, we'd moved to his bed. Now I slipped out, careful not to trip over the cords for his *six* computers as I padded quietly into the bathroom. As soon as I got there I shut the door behind me, leaned against it, and felt the mortification color my cheeks. The truth is, I never go to bed with a guy on the first date (which probably accounts a lot for that eighteen percent), and I had no excuse in this case, where I knew—I mean, really *knew*—that Mike wasn't a guy with long-term potential. Not to mention the fact that I already had my sights set on another guy.

And that, of course, was the other reason I felt like an idiot. And by *that* I mean Cullen and the whole sordid plan. A plan that seemed all the more sordid in the wake of postcoital bliss. After all, I'd originally concocted the Cullen plan in order to up my eighteen percent. And although Mike and I hadn't exactly hung from the ceiling—and although neither nipple rings nor strings of pearls had come anywhere near the bed with us—I still had to say that I was pretty damn satisfied. Did I really need those extra slut-score increasing tricks?

Of course not.

Or, maybe I did. Because I wasn't about to let good sex lull me into starting something with Mike. I'd done that with Dex, and we'd nosedived from quite good between the sheets to wham-bam-thank-you-ma'am to so long, sayonara, and good-night.

Not my ideal scenario. Especially considering the repartee between us had died both sexually and conversationally. It had been slow, painful and heartbreaking. And not something I cared to repeat.

In other words, this night with Mike had been wonderful, but I didn't think my heart could stand having it be more than a one-off.

I paced, eyeing myself sideways in the bathroom mirror as I ran through this conversation with myself. The truth was, self-preservation demanded that I leave now, and leave fast. Okay, fine. I knew my limits, and I knew that there was no way my heart could stand a repeat of the whole Dexter fiasco.

Fine.

But even if that weren't the case, there were other considerations at work here. Specifically, there was phase two of the Cullen plan. A television show. A screenplay. A reason for seduction more noble than a failing grade on a slut test.

"You're pathetic," I whispered to my reflection. Yes, the whole Shag A Model For Your Career Plan had a certain ring to it, but who was I kidding?

I mean, yes, the deal that Carla had scraped up had potential. And yes, I was willing to do pretty much anything in order to further my career. Even Mike would approve of that, right? He was the one who'd said I needed to look for those exits on the highway of life. Exits that—if followed—got me where I wanted to go.

The problem was that this particular exit was littered with nails, potholes and construction delays. Probably carrying a metaphor too far, but it was the truth. The idea that seducing Cullen would lead to a television gig… Well, I'd taken plenty of logic classes in college, and I just wasn't seeing a legitimate cause-and-effect relationship there.

Botton line, even if I did end up in Cullen's bed— and even if I did write a brilliant screenplay—there was no guarantee that Timothy would buy it from me. No guarantee the show would get made.

So, honestly, what was the point? I'd be throwing myself on Cullen for nothing. And I wasn't sure that was a risk I wanted to take.

I closed my eyes and breathed in deep. This wasn't

An Important Message from the Editors

Dear Reader,

*Because you've chosen to read one of our fine romance novels, we'd like to say "thank you!" And, as a **special** way to thank you, we've selected <u>two more</u> of the books you love so well **plus** two exciting Mystery Gifts to send you — absolutely <u>FREE</u>!*

Please enjoy them with our compliments...

Pam Powers

Lift here

Peel off seal and place inside...

How to validate your Editor's
"Thank You"
FREE GIFTS

1. Peel off gift seal from front cover. Place it in space provided at right. This automatically entitles you to receive 2 FREE BOOKS and 2 FREE mystery gifts.

2. Send back this card and you'll get 2 new Harlequin® *Blaze®* novels. These books have a cover price of $4.75 or more each in the U.S. and $5.75 or more each in Canada, but they are yours to keep absolutely free.

3. There's no catch. You're under no obligation to buy anything. We charge nothing—ZERO—for your first shipment. And you don't have to make any minimum number of purchases— not even one!

4. The fact is, thousands of readers enjoy receiving their books by mail from The Harlequin Reader Service®. They enjoy the convenience of home delivery...they like getting the best new novels at discount prices BEFORE they're available in stores... and they love their Reader to Reader subscriber newsletter featuring author news, special book offers, book reviews and much more!

5. We hope that after receiving your free books you'll want to remain a subscriber. But the choice is yours— to continue or cancel, any time at all! So why not take us up on our invitation, with no risk of any kind. You'll be glad you did!

GET TWO *Free* MYSTERY GIFTS...

SURPRISE MYSTERY GIFTS COULD BE YOURS **FREE** AS A SPECIAL "THANK YOU" FROM THE EDITORS

The Editor's "Thank You" Free Gifts Include:

- *Two NEW Romance novels!*
- *Two exciting mystery gifts!*

▼ DETACH AND MAIL CARD TODAY! ▼

Yes! I have placed my

Editor's "Thank You" seal in the
space provided at right. Please
send me 2 free books and
2 free mystery gifts. I
understand I am under no
obligation to purchase any
books, as explained on the
back and on the opposite page.

PLACE
FREE GIFTS
SEAL
HERE

351 HDL EFWG   151 HDL EFZ5

FIRST NAME   LAST NAME

ADDRESS

APT.#   CITY

STATE/PROV.   ZIP/POSTAL CODE

(H-B-08/06)

Thank You!

Offer limited to one per household and not valid to current Harlequin®
Blaze® subscribers.

Your Privacy — Harlequin Books is committed to protecting your privacy. Our Privacy Policy
is available online at www.eharlequin.com or upon request from the Harlequin Reader
Service. From time to time we make our lists of customers available to reputable firms who
may have a product or service of interest to you. If you would prefer for us not to share your
name and address, please check here. ☐

© 2003 HARLEQUIN ENTERPRISES LTD.
® and ™ are trademarks owned and used by the trademark owner and/or its licensee

The Harlequin Reader Service® — Here's How It Works:

Accepting your 2 free books and 2 free mystery gifts places you under no obligation to buy anything. You may keep the books and gifts and return the shipping statement marked "cancel." If you do not cancel, about a month later we'll send you 6 additional books and bill you just $3.99 each in the U.S., or $4.47 each in Canada, plus 25¢ shipping & handling per book and applicable taxes if any.* That's the complete price and — compared to cover prices starting from $4.75 each in the U.S. and $5.75 each in Canada — it's quite a bargain! You may cancel at any time, but if you choose to continue, every month we'll send you 6 more books, which you may either purchase at the discount price or return to us and cancel your subscription.

*Terms and prices subject to change without notice. Sales tax applicable in N.Y. Canadian residents will be charged applicable provincial taxes and GST. All orders subject to approval. Credit or debit balances in a customer's account(s) may be offset by any other outstanding balance owed by or to the customer. Please allow 4 to 6 weeks for delivery.

If offer card is missing write to: The Harlequin Reader Service, 3010 Walden Ave., P.O. Box 1867, Buffalo, NY 14240-9952

BUSINESS REPLY MAIL
FIRST-CLASS MAIL   PERMIT NO. 717-003   BUFFALO, NY

POSTAGE WILL BE PAID BY ADDRESSEE

HARLEQUIN READER SERVICE
3010 WALDEN AVE
PO BOX 1867
BUFFALO NY 14240-9952

NO POSTAGE
NECESSARY
IF MAILED
IN THE
UNITED STATES

a situation I could analyze right then. Not when I could still smell Mike's scent on my body and remember the feel of him thrusting inside me.

Get a grip, Mattie. Get a grip and get to work.

Good advice, and I decided to take it.

I finished in the bathroom, then eased out of the bathroom and found my jeans in a heap on the floor of the living room. Mike was still asleep in the bedroom. I could see the gentle rise and fall of his chest.

I knew I should go say goodbye, but I honestly wasn't up for the mandatory morning-after conversation. Instead, I left him a note.

Had fun. Had to run to the office. Didn't have the heart to wake you.

Didn't have the guts either, but I didn't write that.

And then I crept out the door and fumbled my way into my own apartment.

The second I stepped inside, I knew that was a mistake. I'd forgotten about Angie, who was sitting on my couch, her laptop open with a stack of market reports piled up beside her.

"Morning," she said. "I trust you had a nice night."

"As a matter of fact, I did." I hurried toward the bedroom. "And now I'm incredibly late. I'm going to hop in the shower and get out of here."

"Mmm."

I wasn't sure if that was it, but I didn't wait to find out. Just charged ahead.

I should have known better. A closed door means nothing to Angie. A little fact that I was reminded of about three minutes later when she walked in. Since I was naked and covered with suds, I have to say that she had the conversational upper hand.

"You're going to stop this silly Cullen thing now, right?"

"Angie…" In truth, I pretty much *had* planned to stop it. But I hated the idea of Angie thinking the idea had originated with her.

"I mean, you slept with the guy," she continued. "Mike, I mean. Not Cullen. And he's a really nice guy. And he likes you. And—"

"Enough!" I said, then dove under the water to rinse my hair and give myself just a second of peace. "And this isn't about Mike," I said when I came out for air. "He's a nice guy, and I am attracted to him." *Very* attracted, actually. "But we've hardly professed true love, and for all I know he won't even want to see me again."

"Well, he won't for damn sure if you go after Cullen on that ridiculous scheme of yours!"

That comment knocked a bit of the wind out of me, both because it was probably true and because it bothered me so much. If I didn't want to attach myself permanently to Mike, why should the mere thought that he'd dump me hurt so much?

I didn't have time to think about it, because the phone rang, interrupting our conversation. Or interrupting Angie's lecture, depending on how you wanted to look at it.

Since I figured this was the perfect excuse to avoid the entire topic, I pretty much leaped for the phone, then about had a heart attack when I heard the voice on the other end of the line.

"Mattie! Baby doll! Damn, but it's good to talk to you."

"Timothy?" I swear, my hand was trembling. "Timothy Pierpont?"

"You got it, doll," he said, in that overexuberant voice that seemed to come from deep in his chest.

I knew Carla's boss, of course. I mean, she and I have been attached at the hip for years. So I'd been a fixture at her office holiday party for years. I'd even talked to Timothy once. In the break room. About the eternal debate of straight versus twisty pretzels.

"You there, babe? Suddenly I'm hearing silence. What? Your mouth stuffed full of pretzels?"

"Um, no. I'm here. I'm, you know, just surprised."

"You're surprised. I'm blown away. These pages! Sweetheart, the words leap off the page."

"I…oh, thanks!" I had no idea what project he was talking about, but I'm fast enough on my feet to know that Carla must have slipped him one of my scripts. I wasn't entirely sure if that meant I needed to kiss her or kill her. At the moment, kisses seemed in order, but you could never be sure.

"I don't have the leverage to sell you right now, but you write me up an episode for *Revealed,* and if it's as sharp as this sample, I think we can get something going. You understand what I'm telling you?"

"Yes, sir. Absolutely, sir. And let me just say that I think *Revealed* is a brilliant idea. It's so—"

"Innovative. New. Provocative. I know. My marketing boys have already told me. But that ain't worth shit if I don't have a pilot episode to light a fire under the network executives. Carla says you can deliver. I'm counting on you."

"Yes, sir. Of course, sir. I'll do my—" But he'd hung up, and I closed my mouth, then turned to gape at my sister.

She was shaking her head, a slight grin playing across her mouth.

"Did you catch all of that?" I asked.

"I got the gist of it," she said. "And I know what it means."

"What's that?"

She leaned against the counter. "Any chance I might have had of talking you out of your ridiculous Cullen scheme just died a painful death."

"True enough," I said. And suddenly everything was so clear to me. Timothy had pushed away the mishmash of thoughts that had clouded my brain, leaving the truth shining on me with crystal clarity. And, honestly, I didn't like what I saw. I'd abandoned the law—pissing off my mother in the process—to chase the Hollywood dream. I'd tossed aside years of studying and familial indoctrination to follow my heart.

Except that I wasn't following it anymore. I'd taken huge personal risks those first years, true. But now, at the ripe old age of twenty-seven, I'd become complacent. In my job. In my relationship with Dex. Hell, even in my life.

But no more. Cullen was my answer, and when I looked up at Angie again, I knew my eyes were shining bright with determination.

"This really could be my break," I said. "And there's no way—*no way*—that I'm taking my eyes off the prize."

As SOON AS HE HEARD THE front door click shut, Mike sat up. He'd wanted to roll over and hold her from the moment the change in her breathing had told him she was awake. He hadn't, though. Something in the way she moved had urged him to keep still. A tiny voice in his head telling him that this wasn't the time to press.

Mike had listened to that voice, and he could only hope that it was the angel on his shoulder doing the talking…and not the devil. Because right now, Mike was operating on faith alone. He'd let her walk out even though he was pretty damn certain she was suffering from morning-after regret. If that regret festered—if it lodged in her heart and destroyed any chance he might have of building on the intense attraction between them— well, then Mike was pretty sure he'd have to throttle the source of that little voice. Even if the source was himself.

With a sigh, he rolled over, his hand sweeping the left side of the bed where she'd curled up during the night. In sleep, she'd clung to him, one arm draped across his chest, her fingers gently curled around his arm. Casual and yet possessive. And he recalled with detailed precision the way she'd clung to him when he'd shifted even slightly. His heart had about burst then, and he'd stayed in bed, ignoring the urge for a glass of water, and wanting to comfort her, even if only in sleep.

Not that there had been all that much sleep when

you got right down to it. In actual fact, sleep had been far from it, he thought, as he swung his legs over the side of the bed and sat up. From the first moment his lips had touched hers, Mike had felt as though he could never sleep again. Or eat, for that matter. Why would he have to, when this woman filled him and rejuvenated him? She set him on fire, burned her way through him, and burst him back into life, as jubilant as a phoenix.

He rubbed his hands over his face, shaking his head slightly, amused at his sudden burst of literary license. He couldn't help the way he felt, though. Even before he'd touched her, he'd known. There was just something about Mattie Brown that called to him. And it wasn't simply the fact that she looked damn good in a pair of Levi's, the loose waves of her hair falling over her green eyes as she'd watched him assemble her cabinet. The way her breasts had strained against the threadbare top of the battered bathing suit he'd found her in on Saturday.

Oh, yes. She looked good, all right. But his attraction stemmed from someplace deeper. If he wanted to be literary again—and he really didn't—he'd say that their souls had connected. Undoubtedly, *something* had connected, because Mike had never felt more at home—more perfect—than he had when he'd made love to her.

Even now, when she was no longer in touching distance, he could remember the way she'd felt. The way she'd looked when she'd bucked beneath him, her body glowing with satisfaction.

Later, limp in her arms, he'd wanted to do nothing more than stay awake and gaze at her. His body had betrayed him, though, and, finally, he'd slept.

The pleasure that had lit him before sleeping, however, had faded with the morning. With her quiet, almost guilty, departure from his bed. And now he was faced with the knowledge of knowing that last night had meant more to him than it had to her.

No.

He stood, propelled more by his own intense reaction than by a need to move.

The thought came again, just as firm—*no*. Their encounter *had* meant something to her. He didn't doubt that, couldn't let himself doubt that.

But the truth was, he knew. He simply *knew*. He'd seen it in her eyes. A connection between them. A longing. A need.

But more, he'd seen something real. Something that spoke to him with more force and certainty than her actions. They'd started something in the night.

And even though it might have faded with the rising sun, Mike knew it was there.

All he had to do was find it again.

And that, he thought, was a task worth pursuing.

IT IS A SAD DAY WHEN YOU have to look yourself in the eye and acknowledge that you are, in fact, a complete and total wimp.

That's what I had to do Monday morning. And not just once. No sirree. My wimpiness became apparent twice. And it wasn't even ten yet. Who knew what the day had in store for me?

First, I was wimpy by sneaking out of Mike's apartment without saying goodbye or telling him that our little sex-a-thon was a fluke or even picking a fight.

But I'd already railed on myself enough about that one, so I was just going to let it pass.

Then there came wimpy moment number two. And it, frankly, was the one that really had me irritated with myself. I mean, there I was. All pumped up about writing this damn television show—the producer himself practically promising me that the gig was mine so long as my script didn't bite—and what did I do?

Not a damn thing.

Oh, I tried. I got dressed, raced out of the apartment, and skidded to a stop in front of Cullen's door. But did I knock? Did I say, "Hey, you sexy beast, take me right here, right now?"

No, I did not. I didn't even ask if he wanted to grab a martini that evening. Or coffee right then. Or even fabricate a car emergency and see if he could give me a lift to work on his Harley.

Why did I not do any of those things? Because I am a wimp. Despite all of my big talk about doing what's necessary to get the job done, I am at heart a wimp. (Which could go a long way to explaining why I haven't given John two week's notice, but I wasn't in the mood to think about that.)

The truth was, I couldn't be in a better position. A steady paycheck and an almost surefire "in" into the hallowed halls of screenwriter-dom. All I had to do was make the first move.

This was what I wanted. What I'd *always* wanted.

So why the hell was I dragging my feet?

High on a wave of determination, I pulled up the address book on my computer, found Cullen's number, then picked up the phone. As soon as I heard the ring, the doubt filled me again. What if the blond bimbette answered?

I was riding the crest of that wave, and preparing

to slam down the receiver, when a voice thick with sleep answered.

"Yeah?"

"Cullen?"

"Yeah. Who's this?" He sounded a little more awake now, but his voice still had that sleepy edge. I stifled a little moan as an image of him curled up naked under a sheet flooded my brain.

Except that it wasn't Cullen naked. It was Mike.

Damned uncooperative imagination…

"Hello?" The sleepy voice sounded irritated now.

I shoved the image of Mike out of my head. "It's Mattie," I said. "You know. Your neighbor."

"Right. Hey." The rustling of sheets. "What's up? Other than me?"

I managed a thin laugh, since I wasn't sure if he was playing with me or seriously irritated. "Right. Um. Well. I was just calling to see—"

"You gonna be around tonight?"

I blinked. "Pardon?"

"I've got a late afternoon shoot, but I should be home around ten. So I was wondering if you were going to be around."

"Oh." I sat a little straighter in my seat. This was good. I'd taken the initiative, and it had paid off. I wasn't going to have to ask him out at all. *He* was about to ask *me*. "Absolutely I'll be around." Tonight was the girl-fest that Carla and I had planned—complete with penis pasta salad—but that get-together was scheduled for seven, so surely they'd all be gone by ten. And, if not, they'd understand if I abandoned the lifelike sex toys for the real thing.

"Great," he said. "I'll pop in and grab my mail."

I deflated. "Your mail. Sure. Great. I'll be there."

"Sounds good." He paused, then, "Why'd you call, anyway?"

"Me? Oh, well, I was calling about your mail. I mean," I continued quickly, tripping over myself, my heart pounding in my chest, "I was wondering if maybe you wanted to go get a drink or something. And, you know, if you did, then I could be sure and bring your mail. When, um, we went out, I mean."

"A drink."

My cheeks flamed so hot that I was certain the sprinkler system was going to kick in, drenching me and my idiotic plan. "I just thought, you know, there's that bar on the corner, and I hear the chocolate martinis are good. And we've lived next door to each other for—"

"Sorry, kid. I'm pretty booked. Maybe someday when we're both around we could do something in the moment, though. You know?"

"Oh. Right. Sure." A slow burn edged through my veins. *Rejection? Failure?* I'd never failed in my life, and this was so not sitting well. "I understand," I said coldly, my words clipped. I understood, all right. I didn't have the perky boobs, rock-hard abs and perfectly proportioned thighs of his camera-ready girlfriends. I'd show him, though. Somehow I'd get him on a date, and I'd show him just how much fun a woman with more human than silicone could be.

"Mattie? You there?" His tone was innocent. Oblivious. If he knew he'd pissed me off, he showed no sign. And probably best I didn't rip him a new one right then. That probably wouldn't bode well for future dating prospects.

"I'm here," I said, my tone sickly sweet. "So I'll see you tonight when you get your mail. Sounds good."

"Awesome. You're a doll. Later."

And then he hung up. "Later," I said to the dead line. And then, I said, "Damn."

"Mattie?"

I looked up midbang to find my assistant, Jenny, standing in my doorway. "What?" I snapped.

"I was going to ask you the same thing."

"I was just mourning my utterly pathetic wardrobe." True enough. Because I'd just realized that my first opportunity to show Cullen what he was missing would be tonight. He was coming over, after all. Which meant that he needed to see me in something other than my usual jeans and UCLA T-shirt.

"Oh," Jenny said, in the kind of voice you use around crazy people. Since it's a bad idea to have your staff think you're losing it, I pulled myself together and looked up at her.

"I'm fine, Jenny. Just thinking about this evening."

"Right. Do you need me to pick anything up? Soda? Wine?"

Jenny's a friend as well as my assistant, and she'd been tops on my list of invitees. She's barely twenty-one, and innocent as hell, but considering my pathetic slut score, I figured I couldn't judge. Plus, I'd wanted someone else at the party who was reasonably inexperienced. Call it self-preservation.

I told her I had it all covered, then grabbed my mouse. I intended to spend the morning looking busy when really I was searching the Internet for an outfit I could pick up during my lunch hour. Not my usual modus operandi, to be sure. I rarely sluffed off at work, primarily because I rarely had time. As the point person on all things business-related at the company, I was constantly reviewing contracts, making deals, negotiating pay scales, and interfacing with everyone from the line producers to the union reps. Online shopping never showed up on my agenda.

Today, though, I was happily clicking over to Bluefly.com.

Jenny just stayed there, standing like a statue in my doorway.

"Do you need something else?"

"Actually, yes. The intercom's not working, and you have a call."

I rubbed my temples, not up for the lecture about how she should have mentioned that first thing. "Fine," I said. "I'll take it now. Unless it's Amanda Baker calling to bitch about last week's episode. In that case, just make up some excuse because I'm really not in the mood." Amanda Baker was one of the Talbot twins. You might remember them if you were an adolescent in the eighties. Those overly adorable mystery-solving twins. Like Nancy Drew, only with bigger hair.

After the show's two-year run, though, little Amanda didn't have much luck staying employed (unlike her television sister who now has two Emmys and an Oscar). She'd originally jumped when her agent told her about John's offer. But I think she's finally clued in to the fact that John Layman reality shows aren't exactly warm and fuzzy representations of the daily life of former child stars. The real clue for Amanda was probably when the cameras followed her into the bathroom at one of L.A.'s hipper clubs, thereby messing up her planned heroin deal. (Which, of course, Amanda says was never going to happen in the first place.)

I mean, really. How did I get myself mixed up in this?

"It's not Amanda," Jenny said. "It's someone named Mike. I told him you were on the phone and that I could take a message, but he said he wanted to wait."

"Mike?" Before I could control the reaction, my heart did a little skittering number. I forced myself to calm down even as I forced myself *not* to picture him naked again. Even though it really was a nice picture…

"Right. So, are you here?"

Physically, yes. Mentally, I wasn't so sure. This was the guy whose apartment I had snuck out of that morning…after having had a perfectly wonderful time in his bed just hours before. Was he calling because of the wonderful? Or because of the sneaking?

"Well?"

I sucked up my courage, then leaned over and punched the button for line two. "Mike," I said brightly. "Sorry to keep you waiting."

"I was half-afraid you were going to sneak out of the office without talking to me."

Ouch. Okay, so now my cheeks were flaming again.

"I'm sorry about that," I said. "You were asleep, and I didn't want to—"

"It's okay," he said, cutting me off.

"It is?"

"Sure. I understand."

I sincerely doubted that he did, but I wasn't about to argue the point. Instead, I decided to shift gears as quickly as possible. "So, what's up?" Of course, it could be that he'd called simply to bust me for sneaking out. But since that didn't seem very Mike-like, I took the risk. Besides, I didn't know what else to say.

Jenny was still in the doorway, and I made a shooing gesture. She rolled her eyes, knowing full well that in ten short minutes I'd be giving her a blow-by-blow of the situation and the conversation as we walked down to the lobby for coffee.

I realized that he'd been talking, but my angst had been so loud that I couldn't hear him. "I'm sorry. I didn't catch that."

"I was wondering if we could have lunch," he repeated.

"Oh." A little trill ran up my spine. I forcefully shoved it back down. I needed to keep focused—and my tunnel vision was aimed directly at Cullen. "I'd love to," I said. "But I have plans." A true, if wimpy, response. Because I did have plans. I was spending lunch shopping for an outfit sufficient to catch Cullen's attention.

"My misfortune," he said. "How about after work?"

"Mike…" I drummed my fingers on a contract I needed to wrap up. I was supposed to give the director's agent a return call, but now I wasn't in the mood for playing hardball.

"Come on, Mattie Brown. Last time I saw you, you were naked in my sheets. Surely after that you can find some time for a quick drink. Clothing optional, of course."

I couldn't help it; I laughed. There was something about the man that lifted my mood—even when I was trying to blow him off.

"So is that a yes?"

"I'm sorry, Mike. I really can't. I have plans tonight, too. Some of the girls are coming over. We have…a thing."

"A thing," he said, with a hint of a tease in his voice. "I'm jealous. I always wanted to have a thing."

I muffled a laugh.

"Did you say something?"

"No," I said, holding back giggles. "But I could. And it wouldn't be clean."

"Well, you're off the hook tonight. But only because I refuse to be the one to pull you away from your thing. But how about later this week?"

"Um…"

"I'll spring for dinner. Maybe even another *Thin Man* movie."

"Wow," I said. "You do drive a hard bargain." And even though I *knew* I should say no, I opened my mouth and said, "I guess I could do Saturday."

"Great," he said. "I'm looking forward to it."

"Me, too," I said, both relieved and confused when I realized just how true that statement was.

He clicked off, and I stared at the phone, then returned to my old standby of banging my head on the desk. I should have politely declined, then gone over to his apartment one afternoon and gently yet firmly pulled the plug on this. As it was, I was leading him on.

I gnawed on my lower lip, annoyed with myself, even as my fingers reached for the phone. I could call him back. Cancel the plans. Quickly and firmly dump his cute little ass.

But I didn't. I just couldn't bring myself to make the call. Not then. Maybe not for a while.

So I crossed my fingers, sighed, and wondered if I was going to hell.

Eventually, maybe. But not yet.

First, I was going to Nordstrom's.

7

Penis Pasta Salad
 1 can tuna or diced chicken
 Mayo to taste (couple of tablespoons)
 1 cup diced celery
 8 oz. penis pasta, cooked and drained
 1/4 cup chopped onion
 1/4 cup chopped dill pickle
 Combine ingredients and chill for at least an
 hour.

I ARRIVED HOME ABOUT SIX-FIFTEEN (incredibly early for me on a workday), shopping bag in hand, to a sight that I really didn't want. My bikini-clad sister chatting up Mike by the side of the pool.

I waved from the upstairs landing, and Mike turned and looked at me, his expression softening and pleasure shining clear in his eyes. Angie waved, too, not the least bit guilty. Which, I suppose, made sense.

It wasn't as if she had anything to be guilty about. She was just talking to the guy. I was just feeling jealous.

I blinked at the thought, then stuck my brain in rewind. No, no, *no*. I was *not* feeling jealous! I was just...

I let my thoughts drift off because I couldn't think of what I was "just" doing. And since I didn't want to stand there above them looking baffled, I hurried inside. On the whole, I was a little shook up, but I think I held it together perfectly well. Especially since I didn't have any reason to be shook up.

Jealous, indeed!

I found Carla already in my apartment, boiling water for the pasta and setting wineglasses and cocktail napkins on my dining room table. She immediately started in on how Timothy thought I hung the moon, and how he couldn't wait to read the script, and how she was so thrilled that things were finally moving in the right direction for me.

Honestly, she made me feel like the script was already written and the deal was already done. I stood there for a second, basking in the glow of my brilliant life-to-be, and patting myself on the back for choosing to go after the gold ring, even if Cullen wasn't exactly on board with my plan yet.

I also felt a tiny twang of regret, but shoved it

down. The regret had a big glowing neon label on it—*Mike*—but I reminded myself that I needed to be focused and diligent.

Yup. *Focused* and *diligent* were my new buzzwords.

"Mattie?"

I looked up at Carla, then realized I'd drifted off a bit. "Sorry," I said. "Mind wandering."

"Well, wander in here, would you? Everyone's going to be here in just a few."

I held up the shopping bag. "Give me a sec. Must change. Cullen's coming over tonight, and I want to look like a woman who could be on his arm."

That got her all excited, but I quickly set her right. No, I didn't have a date. Yes, I intended to look damn good in order to promote future date potential.

When I emerged a few minutes later, I knew I looked hot. A darling little low-cut top—the kind that looks almost-but-not-quite like lingerie—paired with black capris. On the whole, I don't like my hair (too brown, too limp), but I'd gelled it and curled it into submission, then pulled it up into a clip, with just a few tendrils hanging loose for effect.

I had mascara, eyeliner and coral-pink lips. And—just for added effect—a tiny hint of Obsession.

All in all, I was enjoying a moment of supreme satisfaction. Rare for one of the female persuasion,

I know. But occasionally it's possible to overcome X-chromosome-induced self-loathing.

When I came back in, Carla whistled, then handed me a screaming orgasm. If that's not the way to start a party, I don't know what is.

As she finished stirring the pasta salad, I sipped the drink and caught her up on everything. And, yes, I mean everything.

She skimmed over my initial Cullen failure, but zeroed in on the whole Mike thing. "Interesting," she said.

"Don't even go there," I retorted. "It's Cullen that Timothy wants front and center. Cullen and the male model glamour factor he can bring to the show."

"Don't jump on me," Carla said. "I only said the situation was interesting. And it is. Even you can't deny that."

No, I couldn't. But *interesting* wasn't exactly the word I would have chosen. Then again, maybe it was the perfect word. Isn't there a Chinese curse? May you live in interesting times. Or something like that.

That thought was worthy of another drink, which I quickly guzzled. In fact, by the time everyone arrived, I'd had two screaming orgasms and found myself staring with fascination at Carla's penis pasta salad. Interestingly enough, penis pasta salad looks remarkably like regular pasta salad, and I wondered if the taste would be similar, too. Of course, after the screaming orgasms, I'm not sure I cared all that much. I *did* care about the way my stomach was spinning, though. Which meant that, obscene or not, food was on the agenda. I jabbed my fork into my bowl, and shoveled a jumble of penises, tuna and mayo into my mouth. I felt a little bit like Gloria Steinem—feminism goes culinary.

At any rate, it tasted great.

Although the party had morphed into Girls' Night Out, it had started from Carla's very pragmatic observation that if I was clumsy with a condom, other girls probably were, too. She'd named it The Penis Party, and the thing had taken off from there. Apparently Carla had really gotten into the spirit, because my apartment had been decked out in a variety of Slut IQ accoutrements. As I parked myself on the couch and faced my massive oak entertainment center, I gazed in wonder at a string of brightly lit penises, like some heretical post-Christmas nightmare. Naughty napkins and paper plates were scattered on my coffee table, which also sported two cinnamon-scented penis candles. Like oversize confetti, a dozen little foil packets decorated the tabletop.

When Carla snags a theme, she sticks with it.

The invited guests arrived in a cluster, with Angie bringing up the rear, a sarong wrapped around her tiny waist, and her breasts (borne of genes not in my family tree) were held up by the skimpiest of bikini tops. I wanted to pull her aside and grill her about her conversation with Mike, but there simply wasn't time. Considering how fast the party was moving, in fact, it didn't even occur to me to argue with myself about my motivation for wanting to question Angie, or to remind myself that I needed to avoid all Mike-related thoughts.

All in all, we were a small but determined group. Jenny had arrived first, which didn't surprise me. She's the only woman I know who scored even lower than me on the slut test. Like me, she was hoping to walk away with a few pointers. Susan Lowell did just fine on the test, but never turned down a party. Greg Martin was here to give a guy perspective on our acquired skills. Carla, of course, was Carla. And Angie was… Honestly, I don't know. For the most part, I think my sister was just amused.

The object of our lesson had a place of honor right in the middle of the table. It sat there, in all its pink, phallic glory, just waiting for a cluster of mostly neurotic women to practice the fine art of sheathing.

"That's the last of the vodka," Greg called from the kitchen. "What did I tell you?"

"I know. Sorry." Greg had ordered me to buy extra vodka on my way home, but I'd forgotten.

On her fourth orgasm, Jenny swayed a little as she came over to stand in front of me. She plucked up a condom and eyed the Love Bunny suspiciously. "I don't think I can do this without another drink."

"You think *you* can't?" Susan sank down into my overstuffed armchair, leaned back and crossed her legs. "Honey, believe me. If I have to drink Diet Coke, I am *so* out of here."

Carla and Greg, our self-appointed den mom and pop, shared a quick look before Greg held up his hand. "Girls, girls, this is not a crisis. I'll just run to the corner and stock up." He waggled a finger at me. "Let this be a lesson to you."

I nodded, appropriately chastised and partially drunk.

One of the benefits of living near a major street was that I was mere minutes from the corner liquor store. Greg could load up on liquor, get back, and we'd barely even notice that he'd been gone.

He checked his hair in my mirror, then pointed to us each in turn. "You, you and you. Sit there," he said, indicating the floor behind the couch. We dutifully marched around the couch and plopped our butts down on the Berber carpet.

He turned to Carla. "You, sit there." She did, sitting cross-legged with her back to the door in front of the semicircle made up of me, Jenny and Susan. Greg passed Carla the Bunny, and she balanced it end-up on her crossed ankles. I thought she looked like some ancient fertility goddess on a bad day, then wondered if I'd drunk too much or too little.

Greg disappeared out the door, and Carla shifted into business mode. "Okay, ladies, who's going first?"

Susan waved toward me and Jenny. "These two are the ones in need of tutoring. I'm just here for the orgasms."

"Well, I can't," Jenny said. "I mean, I just can't. I'm not good at touching his…his…you know." She squinched her face up and waved her hand as if trying to force herself to swallow some really nasty medicine.

I was silently grateful for my eighteen percent. Clearly, it beat the hell out of six.

Carla leaned forward, her hands locked firmly around Mr. Bunny. "Jen, you have to touch it. Sex is a contact sport."

"Not with my hands, I don't." Jenny swallowed the rest of her orgasm, then leaned back against the couch. "I mean, I want to…that's why I'm here. I just never manage to…when we're…and then he gives up and just does it himself."

Susan reached out for Mr. Bunny. "Honey, there's nothing to it. I'll show you."

Carla shrugged and passed Susan the Bunny. With one hand, Susan opened the foil packet and pulled out the condom. Then, with an amazing display of tongue dexterity, she managed to sheath Mr. Bunny using only her mouth. To say I was impressed would be like saying that the Concorde was a really fast plane.

Jenny's eyes widened to comic book proportions. "I can't do that."

"Can you tie a cherry stem into a knot with your tongue?" I asked Susan.

"Cherry stems are the least of my talents."

"I bet," Carla said.

"I absolutely cannot do that," Jenny repeated, now looking a little green. "What if I missed? What if I accidentally bite something important?"

My sentiments exactly. Slut-skill or not, my first priority had to be keeping my guy—and all his moving parts—in working order.

"I can put it on with my toes," Carla—ever competitive—volunteered.

"But why would you want to?" I countered.

"Some guys like feet."

"Feet?" Jenny repeated, her voice rising to near

hysterical levels. "No way. I can't do this. I might as well—"

"My point," Susan said, staring Jenny down, "is that if *I* can do it with my mouth," she nodded toward Carla, "and *she* can do it with her feet, then *you* can do it with your fingers." She unsheathed the Bunny, wiped him clean with a naughty napkin, then passed it on to Jenny. "So try."

Like a trouper, Jenny sucked in a breath, balanced Mr. Bunny between her feet, and opened a lime green packet. The performance wouldn't get her cast in a porno flick anytime soon, but she did manage to sheath the Bunny without doing any apparent injury. She looked up at me, pure delight reflected in her eyes. "I did it! I really did it." She squared her shoulders and sat up a little straighter, secure in her knowledge that now there was only one incompetent condom clod in the room.

Me.

"Your turn," Carla said.

Jenny passed me Mr. Bunny, and I gingerly held it near the base. How hard could it be? After all, there had to be thousands of guys and girls out in the world right at that very moment doing exactly what I was about to do—except not to a Bunny, of course.

I could do this. No problem. I had the key job at

one of the busiest production companies in Holly-wood. I had an expense account. I negotiated option clauses for breakfast. I make a really mean chocolate cheesecake.

I could damn well put on a condom.

Following Susan's lead, I held the Bunny in one hand and tried to open the packet with my other. No such luck. But after a little tooth involvement, I managed to pull out the little latex disk—ribbed for extra sensitivity—and slipped it over the very tippy-top of Mr. Bunny.

So far, so good. I figured I was on a roll.

Then I shifted the Bunny to get a better grip and accidentally hit the on switch. Not a smooth move. Suddenly, I was holding a buzzing, writhing Love Bunny.

Startled, I flung it onto the floor and scooted backward. Carla, Jenny and Susan followed suit, all of us staring bug-eyed at the pastel pink, condom-topped, battery-operated device thrumming and jiggling on my carpet like something out of a porno-horror film. All except Angie, who stayed perfectly in place, a look of amused horror on her face.

The door opened and Greg stepped in, loaded down with a bottle-filled box. "I decided to stock up. Consider it my contribution to the cause." Then he looked straight at me and mouthed, *you've got company.* I blinked, trying to figure out what he meant. And that's when I saw it. One quick glimpse of white T-shirt and tanned skin right there behind Greg. My stomach dropped down to somewhere below my knees.

Oh, shit. I looked around my penis-festooned apartment. Martha Stewart would *so* not approve.

"The shoot ended early," Cullen said, the low tones of his voice coming from somewhere behind Greg. "So I thought I'd grab my mail."

No time for quibbling—I knew exactly what I had to do. In one fluid motion I launched myself up and out, landing with a splat on top of the writhing Love Bunny, just as Slater sidled through the door.

OKAY, CAN I JUST SAY FOR the record that it is impossible to be cool, calm, sophisticated and in control if you are lying prone over a buzzing vibrator topped with a pink rubber bunny?

No, really.

But I put solid effort into it! I really did. And I even managed not to burst into flames of humiliation when Cullen stepped into the apartment, looked around, and then grinned. Slow and sexy and utterly amused.

A woman—tall and slinky and decked out in skin-tight pants and a low-cut knit top—glided in behind him. She took one look around, lifted a perfectly plucked eyebrow, and then cast her gaze on me. I could practically hear her thoughts—*loser!*

Cullen, thank goodness, didn't say anything, and I focused on him, trying to ignore the statuesque, disapproving goddess by my front door. I climbed to my feet, tried to salvage some dignity as I switched the vibrator off, then marched to my desk and the pile of Cullen's mail. I handed it to him with a sweet smile. "Thanks," he said, and as he took the mail, his fingers brushed against mine. He looked me in the eyes, his warm and soft. If this were a script, the writer would say he had bedroom eyes. I didn't say anything at all, just nodded politely when Cullen said, "Yeah. Thanks."

I let my eyes follow him as he swaggered toward the door, hooked an arm around Blondie, then sidled out—just as Mike sidled in, his expression bemused.

"I like what you've done to the place," he said, his eyes drifting from a string of penis lights, to the overall decor of the apartment, and then straight to me. "I had no idea your home decorating style ran to neophallic."

He spoke with a perfectly deadpan manner, and I burst out laughing. Honestly, the guy just did that to me.

"Actually, it's Early American Smut. I'm surprised you didn't recognize the pornographic influences right away."

The corner of his mouth twitched, but he didn't say anything. Instead he took a step toward me. Then another. Until he was so close that my nose tingled from the soapy scent of his shampoo. He put a hand on my shoulder, the gesture friendly and not at all possessive. Even so, I felt possessed. Possessed, and turned-on, and very confused.

"We're still on for Saturday, right?"

I nodded, mute.

He took another look around my apartment, eyes dancing with mirth. Then he nodded to my friends, gave my shoulder a little squeeze, and headed back toward the door. I watched him go, feeling a little sad, actually. Which was absurd. What reason did I have to feel sad? I had a plan in place here. And with any luck, in just a few months I was going to be sitting pretty on a shiny new screenwriting career.

Of course, to get there I needed Cullen to look at me the way Mike did. Actually, that wasn't true. Mike looked at me with something soft and gentle combined with the heat of lust. With Cullen I only needed lust. Hell, when you got right down to it, I only needed sex.

And I could only hope and pray that I hadn't just spoiled my chances with him by throwing myself on a writhing, pink Love Bunny.

IT TOOK ME DAYS TO RECOVER from my Love Bunny fiasco, and during that time I absolutely refused to go outside if there was even the remotest chance of meeting up with Cullen The Wonder Stud. Call me crazy, but there's something particularly appalling about seeing your future boy toy while you're sprawled on top of a squirming vibrator in an apartment filled with penis products.

Not that Slater had demonstrated any interest at all in being a future boy toy. The few times I did see him—from a distance, mind you—he was on the arm of a continually changing parade of women, all who fit into smaller jeans than mine.

That list even included my sister, though I never saw Angie on his arm. I did see them by the pool a couple of times, and once I noticed that he'd helped her change a flat tire. If I hadn't been so mortified about the Bunny fiasco, I might have cared or wondered what my hypercompetitive sister was up to. As it was, I only vaguely hoped she hadn't told Cullen to run far, far away, that I only wanted to use him to further my career.

Assuming I ever got up the courage to talk to him again.

Mike, of course, was a completely different matter. He hadn't seen me sprawled on the writhing vibrator, but he had seen my penis-festooned apartment…and he'd been legitimately amused. No mortification there, and I liked him all the more for it.

Over the last few days, I'd been working killer hours, but I still seemed to see Mike every time I turned around. By the car in the morning, when he was heading off to Starbucks to "fuel up for the day." We'd chat for a few minutes, and then I'd be on my way, a nice little glow hovering over me during my drive to work.

I usually bumped into him by the mailbox, too, in the evenings. On Wednesday, he even had brownies for me, saying he'd picked them up at the bakery and felt the need to share. Since I have to be hog-tied before sharing brownies, this little act of philanthropy touched me, and we'd end up staying down there, perched on the little stone wall that separated the mailboxes from the main walkway.

Looking back, I can't remember what we talked about, but I remember laughing. It was nice. Comfortable. And even though I didn't actually expect to see him there every day, I found myself anticipating picking up the mail. So far, he had yet to disappoint me.

Cullen, unfortunately, was a different animal. He didn't make me laugh, he made me nervous. And I certainly couldn't talk to him the way I talked to Mike.

"It's not fair," I moaned, as I dumped a box of macaroni into a pot of boiling water. "He's the reason I bought the dumb Bunny in the first place." It was as if the universe had played a huge trick on me. Buy the Bunny because of Cullen…avoid Cullen because of the Bunny.

Carla looked up from one of my dog-eared copies of *Variety,* her expression bored. Not surprising—I'd been saying the same thing for days. A one-note wonder, that's me.

"I mean, my dignity's been completely trampled for his sake, and he doesn't even have the decency to know I exist. He only sees women who have silicon implants and streamlined thighs? What's wrong with *that* picture?"

Carla opened her mouth, but I held up a hand to cut her off.

"Never mind. Rhetorical question." I turned my attention back to the macaroni, stirring in nice, even strokes. The thing was, my whole scheme had shifted out of alignment. It was no longer just about my pitiful eighteen percent, or even about the television gig. I wanted to be noticed. And at that particular moment, I was the invisible woman.

I didn't like the feeling one bit.

A tiny voice in my head told me that I was being absurd. That I shouldn't care what Cullen thought. After all, he was paid to look gorgeous, and so were the women he hung around with. They were paper doll cutouts. Not real like me. And Mike, I recalled, hadn't displayed any regret at the size of my thighs. He'd seen me in my bathing suit, and he'd seen me naked. And not once had he run screaming in horror.

Logical, precise and reasonable.

But it didn't make me feel one bit better.

Cullen is the one who'd bruised my ego, and that meant Cullen was the only one who could repair it.

And besides, this wasn't entirely about my ego. If I wanted to get my career on track—and I did—I needed Cullen to notice me. And since that had yet to happen, I was beginning to think that I was going to have to come up with a plan.

A drastic plan.

Fortunately, I already had one in mind.

THE PAPER PANTIES CAME AS a complete surprise.

One second I'd been sitting in the ultraplush

waiting room, my butt planted firmly on some couch that had cushioned derrieres much more high quality than mine. The next second, I was in an equally plush examining room, stripped naked except for my bra and the little paper bikini panties the nurse had shoved into my hand.

Dr. Roger Dodd might be the thigh king, but he was never going to offer Victoria's Secret any serious competition.

Not that I looked even remotely like a Victoria's Secret model. I might be a respectable size ten, but unless I wanted to hire someone to follow me around with an airbrush, there was no way I was ever going to look like the women Cullen Slater invited into his den of iniquity.

Not that I was investigating liposuction solely for the benefit of Cullen. No, this potentiality had been on my mind for a while. Cullen's disdain had simply brought my physical shortcomings into sharp relief.

"Don't you think you're being a little drastic?" Carla had said when I announced my plan to have the fat sucked from my body.

Yeah, well, probably. But wasn't that my new motto? Or close to it at least? Drastic action needed for major life changes?

All of which explains how I'd ended up half-naked

on a Friday afternoon in the examining room of the most high-priced plastic surgeon in Beverly Hills.

One quick rap on the door and Dr. Dodd stepped in. Efficient and decidedly thin, he took one look at me, frowned, and started to scribble on a clipboard. My stomach twisted, and I wondered what test I'd just flunked.

"So," he said, putting down the clipboard, "you're interested in having some work done." He could have just as easily been talking about a Buick, and for some absurd reason my faith in his skill increased tenfold. After all, a doctor with a bedside manner as crappy as this guy's had better be damn good at what he does.

"Um, yeah."

"Breasts?" he continued conversationally.

I shook my head. "Thighs." Bras could be purchased with padding, but there's only so many inches spandex can squeeze away.

His eyes drifted down to my paper panty region, and he began to walk around me, tap-tapping his eraser against the clipboard while I stood there feeling ridiculous. Just when I couldn't stand it anymore, he moved in front of me, looked me in the eyes, and smiled.

"Perfect," he said.

"Excuse me?" I was a long way from perfect.

That's why I was there. If he couldn't see that, I wasn't sure I wanted him designing my new legs.

"You're a perfect candidate for liposuction."

"Oh." I felt better, but confused. "How?"

He began to explain about fat distribution—mine's all in my hips and thighs—and why that was such a good thing. Some women have a layer of fat all over, and it's hard to suck that stuff out. With me—and now he was demonstrating by drawing on my thighs and lower butt with a big, black magic marker—all he had to do was make a couple of incisions, turn on the old vacuum pump and voilà—thin thighs.

By the time he finished his explanation, my stomach was queasy, but my competitive little heart was all aflutter. I might have failed at being a slut, but at least my fat was first rate.

Visions of bikinis and short shorts danced in my head, not to mention men.

Today, Cullen Slater. Tomorrow, the world.

"So what do I do now?" I fantasized that I could plop down on an operating table, take a pill and wake up with model-perfect thighs. On my way home, I'd hit Nordstrom's and buy an entirely new, size six wardrobe. I'd develop a remarkable talent for dancing. I'd be popular, sought after, sexy.

Or not.

Dr. Dodd—my tour guide through fantasyland—steered me toward a few stops along the road of reality. First, he sat me down in a nicely decorated little room with ten photo albums stuffed full of before and after pictures. By this time I was back in my real clothes, although the magic marker marks were still all over my thighs. Nurse I'm-A-Walking-Advertisement-For-Plastic-Surgery sat down with me and we went over pictures of the Amazing Success Stories and the Better-But-Not-Really-Amazing stories.

After I'd been thoroughly warned that the process wasn't infallible—but still reminded that I was a prime candidate for the Amazing Success end of the spectrum—I was steered into Dr. Dodd's actual office for the inevitable How-Much-Are-You-Willing-To-Pay-To-Change-Your-Life talk.

I nearly choked when he quoted me a price.

He shifted into salesman mode. "Of course, that includes all follow-up examinations, medications, any necessary follow-up surgery once the swelling goes down, and the cost of the restrictive girdle."

Girdle? My grandmother wore a girdle. I, however, did not wear a girdle, and I had no intention of cashing in my mutual fund for the privilege of changing that. I must have looked concerned, because he rushed to explain.

"It's temporary. You'll need to wear it for about six weeks after the surgery. It's simply to help your skin shrink to the new you."

In other words, we'd come full circle back to spandex. And four to six weeks? I couldn't exactly get hot and heavy with Slater if I was mummified. I was beginning to wonder if it was worth it. I mean, I'd never be invited to the Playboy mansion, but as far as I knew people weren't covering their eyes and running in terror when I appeared on the beach in a bathing suit.

"You really think I'll see results?" If I was going to fork over serious money, I wanted folks running *toward* me on the beach. I wanted panting males and envious females.

I wanted Cullen Slater wanting me.

"You're a prime candidate." He stood up and casually checked his watch. Clearly my cue to fish or cut bait. "So, Mattie, do you have time this afternoon for the pre-surgery lab workup?"

What the hell? What did I have to lose except my stock portfolio and my fat cells? I opened my mouth to say yes.

"Once you're on the table, we can even pin back those ears at no additional cost."

My mouth snapped shut as my stomach twisted. *My ears?*

True, they stuck out a little. But I never thought anyone actually noticed. Thighs, sure, everyone notices legs. But ears?

Apparently I'd been obsessing over the wrong body part.

My face flushed, my throat closed up, and a few renegade tears tried to make a break for it. I studied the carpet and pulled myself together. When I felt reasonably safe, I coughed, muttered something non-committal, and hoped he couldn't tell that he'd just stomped all over my self-esteem.

Ears. Who would have thought I'd be reduced to a pile of sniffling insecurity because of my ears? Thighs, yes. Tits, undoubtedly. But ears?

A lifetime of self-images started to spin off into oblivion. No longer was I the little girl with the chubby thighs. Now I was the girl with perfect fat, but lousy ears.

It wasn't a pretty picture.

And, truth be told, I wasn't all that certain how much the picture would change after I'd emptied my checking account and put my money where my fat cells were.

I mentally shored up my backbone. The simple fact was, I liked my ears. And I was beginning to get a little pissed off that Dr. Dodd didn't.

For that matter, I was even okay with my thighs. After all, the fat inside them was darn near perfect.

SINCE SHOPPING CURES ALL ILLS, I forced Carla to meet me at the mall after she got off work. I plucked a turquoise blue Barbie shoe off the display. "Do you think these would make my thighs look thinner?"

Carla shot me *the look*, but let it be. "No. They won't even make your ears look flatter." She grinned. "But they do go with the hair."

My thighs might be bulbous, and my ears might be floppy, but, dammit, I had sexy hair. Hair that now did a heck of a job hiding my substandard ears.

According to the mysterious and ever-present *They,* blondes had more fun. Since that's what I wanted, that's what I now was—blond. After the Dr. Dodd fiasco, I'd called the office, said I was sick and would be out the rest of the day, then marched straight to Frederic Fekkai in Beverly Hills. I pleaded and ripped open my checking account to snag an appointment, but it was worth it. After spending the

GNP of a developing nation, I was now the proud owner of lightly permed, subtly highlighted, loose and flowing waves.

I looked fabulous.

And I intended to look better. Which was why Carla and I were prowling the Century City mall in search of a flirty, fun, slimming wardrobe. According to the current *Cosmo,* this year's spring collection was the sexiest ever. So what if it wasn't on sale? With the right pair of Manolo Blahnik shoes and the perfect little black dress, I could completely reinvent myself.

Two hours, three department stores and two venti nonfat lattes later, the stores were closing and our shop-a-thon was wrapping up. Most everything I'd tried on fit, and now I was facing that most dastardly of questions—should I keep the too-adorable-for-words-but-not-really-practical shiny silver pants? Or should I stick with the I'm-a-sexy-career-girl Chanel suit?

Of course, in the end I took the only possible option—I charged it all.

What the hell. It's cheaper than liposuction.

And therapy, too, for that matter.

THE DAMAGE

Liz Claiborne stretch pants and slinky matching jacket

Metallic silver boot pants
Clunky black ankle boots
Chanel print blouse with matching jacket and skirt
Clunky gold Chanel belt
Off-the-rack black skirt
Moshino sundress (ocean pattern)
Denim jacket
Beaded mules
Turquoise Barbie shoes
Manolo Blahnik pumps
Three-pack Hane's V-neck white T-shirts (men's)
Clinique City Base
Estée Lauder Lucidity powder
Estée Lauder Lash Luxe mascara
Lancome Couleur Flash Blush Stick
Fendi zebra-striped evening bag
Kenneth Cole leather purse
The Verdict?
Maybe liposuction would have been cheaper after
   all.

8

ALTHOUGH MY APARTMENT complex is not exactly *Melrose Place,* it does occasionally have its share of drama. I woke Saturday morning, for example, to the sound of something crashing against my west-facing wall. Since that's Cullen's apartment, I immediately got curious. And, yes, I'm ashamed to admit that I leaned against the wall, trying desperately to hear the argument going on next door.

Not that my efforts paid off. A lot of crashing and a shrill female voice followed by Cullen's more baritone tones. Granted, I couldn't tell what was being said, but it was still more engaging than the Saturday morning shows I'd otherwise be listening to.

After a few minutes, I heard Cullen's front door slam, followed by the clatter of heels down the walkway toward the stairs. And then, silence.

I slipped into my robe and padded to the kitchen

to make coffee and wake up Angie. Assuming, that is, that she'd slept through the drama.

The coffee I got on right away. Angie, however, was nowhere to be found, and I assumed that she'd gotten tired of the drama in my complex and had moved to the Four Seasons. I remembered that I hadn't seen her last night, either. Which was fine. Angie's a big girl, and I'd been more than happy hanging out with Carla.

I was tempted to call Carla now, just to report on the neighborly drama, but then I remembered that she and Mitch had headed off to Ojai early that morning. An entire week at a spa. Is it any wonder I envy my best friend's life?

I puttered around for a while, reading the newspaper, drinking coffee, trying to convince myself to head into the office and take care of the teetering stack of papers on my desk. But I couldn't quite work up the enthusiasm. Nor could I get excited about my Cullen plan. I needed to focus on that, figure out how I was going to attract the man's attention. One of yesterday's purchased outfits would be involved, yes, but how? Bump into him casually? Follow him to onepof his clubs?

I didn't know, and I was spending the morning pretending I didn't care. For that matter, I was going to spend the entire day not caring. I had a date with

Mike tonight, after all. And even though this was a friends-only date I still wanted to be rested beforehand. And bathed. And thoroughly moisturized.

Carla might be at a spa, but that didn't mean I couldn't pamper myself, and I intended to start right then.

I got up, planning to search the drawers in my bathroom for the mud mask I'd picked up at this darling little store I'd discovered in Santa Barbara. I didn't make it that far, though, because someone knocked at the door. I opened it without thinking and found myself standing face-to-face with Cullen. Only his face looked fabulous and mine still had sleep-crusty eyes.

"Hey," he said, looking slightly past me. "So, what's shaking?"

"Nothing," I said, warily. "Um, Cullen, why are you here?" Perhaps not the best approach seeing as I wanted to seduce the guy (or have him seduce me) but it was early and I wasn't at my sharpest.

"Sorry. Nothing. Nothing."

Some little demon nudged me, and I peeked out the door, looking toward the stairs. "I heard your door slam. Rough night with the girlfriend?"

"Something like that," he admitted.

"Well, later." I stepped back, starting to close my

door. I just couldn't do fun and flirty in a bathrobe with bed head and morning breath.

Cullen, however, wasn't letting me get away. "So, what are you doing tonight?"

I squinted at him. "Tonight?"

"Yeah. You wanna go get a drink or something?"

"You're asking me out?"

"We could go around the corner. A casual thing." A shoulder lifted, then fell.

I wanted to ask him why he was asking me out on a Saturday night. For a guy like Cullen, that clearly meant sloppy seconds. Or maybe sucky sixths. And I really don't like being second (or eleventh) best.

But I wisely kept my mouth shut. This was my ticket, after all.

True, I was going to have to cancel my date with Mike. But it wasn't a *date* date. And this, after all, was business.

And so, despite my curiosity and my previous plans, I nodded my head and said, simply, "Yes."

"GREAT MUSIC, HUH?" CULLEN bent toward me, shouting over the din of voices and music from the band in the corner. I nodded, wishing I had a magic remote control that would turn the volume down, and tried to smile as if I were having a good time.

On The Boulevard is a local hotspot, just around the corner from our apartment. I'd never been in before, and now I knew why. I much preferred the nice, quiet wine and tapas bar across the street.

The truth was, I didn't like crowds or clubs or eardrum-splitting music. Cullen, apparently, thought this was heaven on earth. I had a feeling that made me the abnormal one, but at that moment, I didn't care. I was too worried about losing all my hearing.

I leaned closer. "Do you want to go get a table? I think there are a few open in the back." Gloriously away from the speakers.

For a second, I thought he'd disagree. Then he nodded. "Yeah. Sure. Whatever." He signaled something to the bartender, who nodded. Then Cullen took my hand and started to lead me toward the back of the bar. It took a while, because he had to chat with every pretty girl along the way, and slap the back of a few guys.

Clearly, I was out with the quarterback, and a tiny part of me wanted to melt into the floor. Because I'm so not the homecoming queen.

But I sucked it up and kept on.

Eventually, we were out of range of the girls he

knew (or, possibly, didn't know but was flirting with anyway). We found a table, and I tried to do the small-talk thing.

Let me just say for the record that it wasn't pretty. It wasn't pretty at all.

I talked. He grunted.

I asked about current events. He glanced distractedly around the room.

I mentioned our landlord. He said an entire sentence in reply. I rejoiced, figuring we'd hit a common ground. I was wrong. The sentence trailed off, and he returned to the land of distracted grunts. Damn.

Then I remembered what all the networking books recommend—talk about him. People, it seems, love to talk about themselves.

So I tried that. I asked him about modeling, about where he was from, and about what he wanted to do ultimately. That time, I hit pay dirt. And even though I can't say I was fully engaged in the conversation, at least we were having one. And, honestly, he was a nice guy. A nice, incredible-looking guy.

No, not just incredible-looking. This guy was smoldering. Carla and I had known that for months. Not that I'd said much more to him in those months other than "Hi," and "Happy to bring in your mail." But a girl picks up on smoldering.

All the women in this bar were proof of that. We'd pretty much had to wade through a sea of female lust just to get to this table. Even now, I could see women around the room eyeing Cullen greedily. And whenever their gazes lit on me, I knew exactly what they were thinking: What was *I* doing with that hunka-hunka burning testosterone?

A good question. And one that wouldn't need to be answered if I was playing this right. I was supposed to be seducing the man. Or at least setting myself up to be seduced.

But was I?

No. I was nursing a vodka tonic, chatting about his modeling gigs, and bemoaning the fact that I wasn't as toned as the women who flowed around us.

Clearly I wasn't cut out for this.

Just as clearly, I needed to try. Crappy reality show job. Screenplay. Ultimate career opportunity. Remember?

I did remember, and so I leaned forward and let my fingers brush across his hands.

He looked at me. Not with heat or interest or even curiosity. Just looked.

"Um, thanks," I said, knocked a bit off-kilter.

"What for?"

"Oh, you know. For bringing me here. It's great."

His brow creased. "Great? I had the feeling you didn't much like it here."

Okaaaaaaay. Maybe I wasn't quite the actress I thought I was.

"I'm just not used to sitting still when there's music playing," I lied.

"Then let's go dance." He stood, his hand outstretched for me, and I had no choice but to go with him. We glided hand in hand through the bar, slipping through clusters of customers, and moving with a determined eagerness.

On the dance floor, Cullen pulled me close, and we moved together, our bodies in tune with the music. He smiled at me once, and I could see in his eyes that my plan was working. Or it could work, anyway. There was potential there, along with a question.

What I didn't know was how to answer it.

And so I ignored it, losing myself in the music and the dance. Cullen was a bump-and-grind kind of guy, and our bodies moved in time together, meshing and molding, swaying and grinding. The music was loud, the beat steady, and the air hot and sultry.

I kept waiting for my body to catch fire. For me to lose myself to sensual need and to demand—even silently—for him to touch me.

But I never got there. I wanted to be touched—yes. But the desire wasn't attached to Cullen. It was loose, vaguer. And right then, I wished that I were alone in my apartment with my Love Bunny.

The thought startled me, and I shoved it away. I'd left my vodka at the table, and now I craved it and the way that another gulp would make me feel loose. I craved loose. I craved desire. I *wanted* to want this man. And I edged closer, telling myself that he was just picking up on my awkward vibe. And as soon as he saw how turned-on I was, everything would shift toward the sensual.

Never mind that I *wasn't* turned-on. Surely that little problem would be eradicated soon enough.

He hooked an arm around my waist and pulled me close. I felt a rush of victory and clung to it, willing it to morph into a rush of sensual need. It didn't. That was okay, though. Cullen was the kind of guy women drooled after. Even *I* drooled after him. So any missing lust feelings had to be due to nerves. Once I had the guy in bed, I was certain it would be bliss all the way.

I pressed closer, my hips conforming to his, our bodies gyrating with the music. I closed my eyes, letting the sounds fill me, letting the bass vibrate through me. I *wanted* this. Wanted to be turned-on. Wanted to lose myself to the moment.

And as I told myself how much I wanted it, my body decided to cooperate. I felt my limbs go warm and my nipples peak. My thighs tingled and my panties dampened. An image filled my mind, and I reached for it, wanting to make it real, wanting to see it clearly.

When I did, I gasped.

Mike.

The man in my fantasies—the man fueling my body's decadent reaction—was Mike Peterson.

Dear Lord, what had I done?

"Mattie?"

Flustered, I looked up into Cullen's eyes. He didn't look offended or amused, just curious. I, of course, felt mortified.

"You stopped dancing."

"Oh." So I had. "Tired, I guess." I hooked a thumb toward the bar. "I'm going to go get some water. I'll be right back."

"Do you want—"

I shook my head, no. I didn't want company. And from the way he was bouncing with the rhythm, I could tell he didn't want to leave.

No problem. I made my escape and begged some ice water from the bartender. He appeared with it, and

I took the glass gratefully, turning back to look at the dance floor and my hunka-hunka burning Cullen.

Didn't see him anywhere.

I frowned and scanned the dance floor, ultimately finding him doing a bump and grind with a leggy blonde. A redhead came up from behind, trying to hone her way into the action. He swung an arm around the girl and kissed her cheek. He obviously knew her (which didn't surprise me; she looked like a model) and whereas he and I hadn't found a thing to talk about, he and Red seemed to be getting along just fine.

I sighed, and waited for a wall of jealousy to slam up against me. When it didn't, I let my gaze float over the crowd. And *that's* when the jealousy hit. Because across the room I saw my sister, leaning in close to talk to a guy who, lately, had been making my pulse race and my palms sweat. *Mike.* Not fifteen feet away.

A hot flash of embarrassment and regret ripped through me. I'd told him I had to work tonight—and while that was *technically* true, I could hardly explain the whole work/Cullen/script thing to Mike.

I forced my emotions back on track by very sternly telling myself that it didn't matter anyway. If Mike was really friend material, he'd get past my little bit of evening-maneuvering. And since I didn't care about him being relationship material…

As I was engaging in this little bit of rationalization, the man in question turned his head, his eyes immediately connecting to mine. I gasped, then tried to pull myself together. This was nothing but a girlie postsex reaction. Mike wasn't the one I wanted. Neither was Cullen, for that matter, but at least banging Cullen would serve the dual purpose of ratcheting up both my slut score and my career.

My brain knew all that, of course, but my libido was sadly uninformed. And when Mike broke away from Angie's side to start walking toward me, I felt my knees go weak. I reached back, clutching the bar with my free hand, and hoped that I didn't look too much in lust.

"Hey," he said.

"Hey yourself."

He signaled the bartender and ordered a beer for himself and "Whatever the lady wants." Since the lady was too much of a wimp to say what she *really* wanted—"Drop to the floor and take me right here"—she ordered a fresh vodka tonic. The bartender went off to do his thing, and Mike focused all his attention on me.

"You looked good out there."

"Oh." I turned to glance at the dance floor, where Cullen was currently bumping uglies with Red. "You, um, saw me?"

"I saw you."

"Mike, I'm sorry. I—"

He waved a hand. "Don't worry about it. We'll have dinner some other night. In the meantime, though, I want you to answer a question."

"Um, sure. What?"

"Are you two dating?"

I narrowed my eyes at him. "Why?"

"After the other night, don't I have a right to know? I mean, the guy looks pretty tough. What if he decides to bash my face in?"

I laughed. "No," I admitted. "We're not dating."

"Glad to hear it."

I didn't say anything. As far as I was concerned, we'd just slid into dangerous territory. But at the same time, his firm response made me feel nice and warm.

"So, you're here with Angie?" The little green jealousy monster popped up again, and I smacked it brutally back down.

"Yeah."

"Oh." I shifted from foot to foot. *I wasn't going to ask. I wasn't going to ask.*

Okay, hell. I asked. "So, is this, like a date?"

He gave me a sideways look, and for a second, I was sure that he was going to say yes. Then he smiled—one of those smiles that taps you in the gut—and said, very simply, "No."

I told myself that the surge of happiness I felt stemmed from the fact that Angie didn't need to be bouncing through men in my apartment complex. She had enough men on a short leash in her own neighborhood!

I told myself that, but I didn't really believe it. But since I didn't care to delve into a deep analysis, I tried to ignore the emotion altogether.

"So how come you happened to end up here?" I asked, this time just for something to say.

"I was doing laundry, and Angie cornered me. Said you'd abandoned her and she was all alone. She said she was going to come down here and get a drink, and since she hinted that she didn't want to go alone…"

I laughed. "In other words, it *is* a date."

He met my eyes, his firm and unyielding. "No," he said again. "It's not."

I swallowed, silent under the force of his words. Then he took my hand and started moving toward the dance floor. "Let's dance."

"I'm not sure if—" But I cut myself off. I did want to dance. At least if we were dancing we wouldn't be talking. Because unlike talking with Cullen, talking with Mike was a tingly kind of experience.

MIKE LED MATTIE ONTO THE dance floor, moving expertly through the mass of surging bodies. She'd come without protest, and he was reveling in that fact. More, he was plotting what to do to keep her with him. To keep her protests firmly silenced.

Giant speakers surrounded the scuffed parquet of the dance floor tucked against the far wall of the bar, right in front of a raised platform on which the band sang and gyrated. Apparently they were also playing music, but Mike was having a hard time hearing anything but his own thoughts. Decadent thoughts that were urging him to pull Mattie into his arms, slide his hands over her breasts, thrust his tongue into her warm, soft mouth.

He shook himself, forcing his imagination back into the land of the nonprurient. Now was the time for dancing. The time for seduction was later, God— and Mattie—willing.

The music that he was basically ignoring must have been popular, though, because the floor was jam-packed. Not a bad arrangement, really, because it put Mattie that much closer to him. She was watching him, but clearly trying not to look as if she was watching him, and he made a show of dancing as if his life depended on it. At the moment, he rather thought it did.

Off to one side, he saw Angie, and he had to grin.

He didn't know exactly what was going on with her, but she'd cornered Cullen, and now they were swaying to the music, interlocked in a series of sensual, pulsating thrusts. He thought about copying their moves with Mattie in his arms, and simply from the force of the thought alone, his cock started to twitch. *Damn.* He had it bad.

He also knew that he owed Angie big-time, and when she caught his eye, he smiled. She nodded. Not so much that anyone could see, but just a tiny little bob of her head, a gesture meant only for him.

He grinned. Yes, indeed, Mattie's sister was his new best friend. More, she was his secret weapon.

Because Angie had revealed the secrets of the universe to him. Mike's universe, at least, since of late it seemed to revolve entirely around Mattie. And he'd been beyond thrilled to learn that Angie hadn't been kidding when she'd cryptically told him that Mattie's interest in Cullen was for show. It was.

Mike was still a little unclear on why Angie wanted to get involved. Whether she simply wanted to hook Mike and Mattie up, or whether she had an agenda of her own. Either way, Mike didn't care. He was just happy to learn that Mattie's fascination for their buff neighbor tied in with screenplays and television deals and Internet slut tests. That was all well and good (if a bit bizarre), but what had really piqued Mike's interest was the underlying suggestion that Mattie's fascination with Cullen stemmed from his bad-boy attitude.

Mike, Angie explained, was a good guy. Nice. Helpful. The kind of guy who returned your margarita glass and assembled furniture. Not the kind of guy who screwed you brainless in the backseat of a Thunderbird. (And, yes, she'd really said that. Mike had to give the girl her props.)

In short, Mike was too much like Mattie's ex to be in the running for boyfriend material.

And although Mike had been too flabbergasted to respond to Mattie's sister, he was sufficiently recovered enough to now respond to the woman herself. Yes, he was a bit of a geek. But before this night was over, Mike intended to show Mattie that he was one geek who had nothing in common with Dex. Because Mike had at his fingertips a full repertoire of sensual delights…and knew at least a dozen ways to please a woman. In *and* out of the backseat of a Thunderbird.

I HAVE OFFICIALLY CHANGED MY mind about live music and dancing. Out on the floor with Mike, it didn't seem so much an obnoxious din, but a blanket of sound that carried me away. And can I also say that for a geek (albeit an incredibly good-looking geek), the man can *dance*.

Not that I got to see too many of his moves. Because right away, he maneuvered us toward a corner, where some large wooden pedestals had been set up for people to dance on. He didn't—thank goodness—maneuver us onto the pedestals to dance *American Bandstand* style, but he did scooch us up so close that any expectations I might have had of personal space evaporated.

Honestly, I didn't mind too much.

The corner was dark, and even though the music was loud and fast, he pulled me close, his arms sliding around me as he led me in a slow dance. I didn't protest; I wanted this, and I was more than happy to blame it on the music and the vodka. Then his hips shifted, and I felt the hard demand of his erection.

I gasped as the world seemed to evaporate under my feet, undone by a wave of lust. And suddenly, I wanted more—so much more—than a simple dance. I had no idea how he could bring me to arousal so quickly. Just a soft brush of bodies and the erotic thrum of music, and I was wet, my crotch tingly, and my nipples straining against the satin of my sexy little top. And all that just from a quick brush of bodies that very easily could have been accidental.

Oh, God, I hoped it *wasn't* accidental.

The thought snuck into my head and I started a bit. Yesterday—or even a few hours ago—I would have quashed the thought, beat it into submission. But right then... Well, right then I wanted that connection. My hormones were in overdrive, and even though common sense and my overanalyzed plan told me that I should run and find Cullen, my body told me that I'd be insane to leave.

I decided to listen to my body. After all, with Mike's help, I was certainly racking up the Internet slut points. Wet on the dance floor...that had to be worth at least five points. Surely I could rack up even more...

To that end, I edged closer, moving in time with the music, but managing to brush up against him as I did. I caught his eye, and saw the heat reflected there, and knew that his own touch had been no accident. This was a man with a plan, and I couldn't wait.

Luckily, I didn't have to. His hands slid around my back, slipping up under the thin material of my shirt to caress my back, causing a sensation in my body that I was afraid would culminate in spontaneous human combustion. He pulled me close, his crotch pressed against mine, and the hard bulge of his erection causing me to go a little weak. He held me up, strong hands caressing me and keeping me close as we swayed, not in time with the music, but with our own song of lust.

He took control, edging us even farther back, until we were almost behind the pedestal, officially off the dance floor and away from the storm of colored lights that swept over the bodies moving on the floor.

My body was on fire just from the thrum of the music and his proximity, but when he slipped his hand down into my jeans, I about dropped to the floor and lost it. I was hot and wet and slick, and I ground against him like a wild thing, grateful for the dark as I clung to him, whimpering slightly as I came in his arms.

Sanity returned slowly, and when it did I knew I ought to be mortified. But I wasn't. I wanted more. So much more, and when I pulled back and looked him in the eyes, I knew that he could tell.

"Come with me," he said.

I didn't hesitate. Just twined my fingers with his and followed him down the dark corridor to the rear women's restroom. He paused there, and I gaped. "Mike, you're not…"

But he just turned the knob and pulled me inside the small room. He flipped on a light, revealing a toilet, sink, and a metal cabinet. The room was small and cramped, but clean, and I wondered vaguely about the women who might need in there. My sympathy for them faded, however, when Mike locked the door and turned to face me, his expression serious. At least until he waggled his eyebrows, effectively releasing all the tension that had built up in inside me. Screw the other women; they could trot across the bar to the restrooms by the front entrance.

He held his arms out in silence, and I slid into them, our lips melting together as hands explored, snaking under clothes, caressing skin, getting us hotter and hotter until I swear I was going to explode or die or melt.

His hand cupped my crotch, and the pressure drove me insane. "Mike." My voice, barely a whisper, reflected the absolute depth of my need. And Mike, bless him, didn't hesitate. He lifted me, then moved across the tidy little bathroom until my rear was pressed against the porcelain of the sink. A bit more fumbling, and suddenly I was naked from the waist down.

Mike disappeared, sliding down my body even as his hands clutched my thighs. I held on to his shoulders, my body trembling as his tongue stroked my clit, driving me up and up until the world exploded around me and my fingers touched heaven.

After I'd come back down to earth, I clutched his shoulders, needing to see him, to feel his lips on mine.

He rose slowly, his eyes on mine, and his lips glistening. I thought about where those lips had just been as I watched him speak to me, my body still trembling with the memory of Mike's intimate kisses. He was saying words, but I was too lost in the moment to translate.

"Mattie?"

My name finally penetrated and I grunted some sort of reply.

"Did you hear me?"

"Nope," I said happily.

"I asked if you wanted to go back to the dance floor. Or head back to my apartment." His finger stroked the wet slit between my legs. Reflexively, I looked around. My panties were half in and half out of the trash can. Good riddance. "Or we could just stay right here." The last he said in a low voice, one hand reaching for the fly of his jeans.

I reached to help him, instinctively spreading my legs wider. "I think I like that option."

Too bad for us, someone chose that moment to pound on the door. I looked at Mike, and he looked at me, and we both started laughing, hands clasped over our mouths to try not to be too loud.

"Just a sec!" I called, as Mike helped me into my clothes. We clung together, holding in laughter, as we slipped out of the bathroom, past the raised eyebrows of the slightly drunk blonde waiting for access. "All yours," I said.

"Him, too?"

"No way," I called back over my shoulder. "I don't do the sharing thing."

We ran out the back door, hand in hand, then raced home. We were like kids, taking turns tugging the other forward, sneaking kisses in the lee of trees, waving at the passing cars.

When we finally reached our apartment complex, we were breathing hard, and we stopped in the laundry room to get a drink from the water cooler.

I gulped about a gallon, then came up for air and grinned at Mike. My playful mood, however, quickly evaporated when I saw the heat in his eyes. He moved slowly toward me and patted the top of the washing machine. "Even better than the sink. This one vibrates."

And then, as I watched, he pulled four quarters from his pocket, fed them into the machine, and started the thing working. Then he raised an eyebrow. "Better than one of those vibrating beds in a cheap motel, huh?"

"You're a nut," I said, utterly enchanted. Surprised, too. Who would have thought that my geeky neighbor would be the guy to ratchet up my point total? And all in the space of one night?

"A nut," he repeated. "Is that a good thing, or a bad thing?"

"Come here," I said. "And I'll tell you after."

I didn't have to ask twice. He came into my arms, and as I opened my mouth to his, I realized how I'd come full circle. My whole sordid plan had started in this laundry room, and now here I was in Mike's arms.

With a start, I remembered Cullen. I'd left him alone in the bar. I felt a quick smattering of guilt, but quashed it. He was a big boy, and I was quite certain he could find his way home.

And at the moment, I wasn't too concerned about etiquette anyway.

MIKE HAD NEVER FELT SO LOST…or so found. He'd made love to Mattie in the laundry room, the sweet intensity of it coming close to driving him mad. And now that she was pressed against him, her arms wrapped around his neck and her breathing coming slow and deep, he knew that he didn't want the moment to end.

From a practical standpoint, though, he also knew they needed to get out of the laundry room. It might be the middle of the night, but there were enough twentysomethings in the complex to make an intimate laundry room tryst a potentially revealing encounter.

He held on to her for a few more seconds, trying to decide what to do. Then he remembered the laundry he'd left tumbling earlier in the day. Now he moved to one of the dryers and pulled out a blanket. "Follow me," he said, reaching for Mattie's hand.

They ended up sharing one of the lounge chairs by the pool, curled up next to each other, the stars dim above their heads, their light mostly overshadowed by the glow of Los Angeles. He'd loved making love to her, but this was somehow even sweeter. Just the two of them, cuddled up, whispering and laughing and talking about anything and everything.

She was friend and lover. And he knew without a doubt that he never wanted to lose her. With a soft little sigh, she slipped her arm around his waist. He leaned in closer, pressing a soft kiss against her hair. And then, with the stars as their witness, he drifted off to sleep.

I WOKE UP WITH THE SUN, which sounds wonderful in theory, but in actual practice, it was a little disconcerting. We were, after all, snuggled together outside, surrounded by twenty-two apartments, all of which had a lovely view from their front window of our snuggle-bunny-ness.

Not exactly a shining moment for me. Even less so

when, as I carefully slid out from under the blanket, I saw Cullen slinking up the stairs to his own apartment, looking just as fresh as he had the night before. I sincerely doubted I looked as good, and I stifled the urge to dive back under the blanket and hide.

I didn't, though, and when Cullen turned and saw me, I gave him a weak wave. A sly grin crossed his face, and his eyebrows rose just an inkling. And the really weird thing? I didn't think he was disturbed or annoyed or otherwise freaked out that I'd abandoned him to go do the nasty with some other guy.

On the contrary. I thought Cullen was a little bit intrigued. And it took supreme effort for me not to buff my fingernails across my chest. I mean, maybe I hadn't screwed up my shot at Timothy's show after all.

For that matter...

I hurried upstairs, the idea fresh on my mind. I entered quietly, but when I realized that Angie wasn't home (*where* was she?), I lunged for the phone to call Carla. I had a brilliant plan, and all I had to do was get her okay to use Mike as the focal point of my script instead of Cullen. I still wasn't ready to think about the possibility that I was truly falling for the man, but I was more than willing to accept that he had more fling potential than I'd given him credit for.

And maybe that could be the theme of the episode—finding hot sex in the unexpected male.

Unfortunately, I didn't get through. Instead, I got her voice mail, naturally (I mean, what did I expect? She was with Mitch!). I left a message to call me, then drummed my fingers on the desk, trying to decide what to do. I wasn't too worried, though. My idea for a shift in the script's perspective seemed brilliant to me. Surely it was the best way to go.

I didn't have much time to ponder that eternal question, though, because I was already running late for work. So I stripped my clothes off, then booted my computer up before running to the shower. Later, I sat clean and damp at my desk, and combed out my hair as I scrolled through my e-mails. My heart skipped a beat as my eye caught one particular e-mail about ten down the list.

I clicked on it eagerly, then swallowed hard as I read Timothy's note.

Mattie, doll!
Carla left without giving me your cell phone number, so I'm resorting to e-mail. Sweetheart, you have done yourself proud. Finished *The Thin Line* last night at 3 a.m., and if you think I stay up until three as a rule, you're dead wrong.

Can't do a damn thing with it now, but down the road...well, that's a different story. You get me a killer script for the pilot, and we'll be in business. I know you can do it. And with Cullen Slater as the focus, I know we can't miss. You've seen the latest issue of *Entertainment Weekly*? He's not on the cover yet, but the boy is going places. And if you snag him (and shag him), I'd bet a week of dinners at Spago that our Nielsen's will go through the roof.

I read the thing through twice, trying to find some way to reconcile the words on the page with my newly formed plan to simply forget about Cullen and pursue my very satisfactory extracurricular activities with Mike.

Unfortunately, I couldn't figure that one out.

And so I decided to take the coward's way out. I shoved the entire situation out of my mind, got dressed, and ran out the door to the office.

I needed something to help me forget my own problems, and the life, loves and drugs of spoiled former child stars seemed like just the ticket.

9

TEN HOURS AND THIRTY-SEVEN minutes later, I realized just how right I'd been. I was in hell. Complete and utter hell, filled with writhing, screaming demons who vaguely resembled human beings but who clearly weren't really human judging by their sincere, earnest and loudly voiced desire to be featured on a reality television show in all their dysfunctional glory.

Thank goodness it was Sunday, so I was dealing with these folks only on paper and by e-mail, going through contracts and answering correspondence.

Clearly, I needed to find a new job. Lucky for me, I had a perfect opportunity just waiting for me. I knew I could do the work justice. I knew that I could write something that totally wowed Timothy. And once I did, the sky was the limit. Because anyone that Timothy cared to anoint was golden in Hollywood.

I looked around my office and sighed. I wanted to

be golden. I'd thought I would be when I took this job. And I'd wasted years. Now I had the chance to make up for lost time.

That meant I needed to pursue Cullen. Not Mike.

And I had to focus. I needed to achieve the kind of results that would land him firmly in the middle of my soon-to-be-written story…not to mention my bed.

I'd known since Carla had told me about Timothy's new series that Cullen was my key to job satisfaction. Timothy's e-mail had simply hit home just how true that was.

Time to get to work.

I closed out all the office-related things on my computer (after all, it was the weekend I could justify some me time) and pulled up Final Draft, my favorite screenwriting software.

The cursor blinked, and I blinked back.

Finally, I typed FADE IN.

Okay. So far, so good.

I tapped my fingers on my desk, waiting for inspiration to hit. When it didn't, I dropped down a line and entered, INT. LAUNDRY ROOM—DAY.

That's where this all started, right? So that's where I had to begin.

I was just about to start typing what I remembered of my original conversation with Carla when the phone rang. I grabbed it without thinking, then immediately regretted that when I heard the low drawl on the other end of the line.

"Hey, gorgeous."

"Mike!" I took a deep breath, reveling a bit in my memory of him.

"I missed you today."

"Yeah," I said. "Me, too." I regretted the words the second they were out of my mouth. Not because they weren't true (they were), but because I couldn't go anywhere with this. Not now, anyway. The whole situation made me a little sad, but I refused to let my focus waver. I'd come to Los Angeles with an intent to conquer, and so far I hadn't done that. I was on a mission here. A mission to make up for lost time.

Plus (and, yes, maybe I was rationalizing a bit), I'd told myself for days now that Mike wasn't long-term material. He was damn good in bed and made me tingle all the way down to my toes, but long-term, he just wasn't Mattie Brown material.

That's what I'd been saying, anyway. And, yes, I'll admit that I'd veered off that intense stand. Mike did have some potential. But potential wasn't the same as a sure thing, and faced with a possible relationship and a surefire entrée into Hollywood… Well, excuse me, but I was going for surefire.

Just call me Pragmatic Girl.

"Mattie?"

"Sorry," I said. "I'm here."

"Glad to hear it. I was beginning to think you'd been swallowed by your desk chair."

"That happens sometimes," I admitted. I smiled and leaned back in my chair, completely comfortable. Talking to Mike was like talking to a good friend. He *was* a good friend. He was also good in bed, which made for a nice overall package.

But there was that one little thing hanging over us…

I cleared my throat. "Listen, Mike…"

"How about dinner," he said, at exactly the same time.

I sat up, no longer leaning back, no longer comfortable. "Dinner," I repeated. And then it hit me. I already knew, of course, but it hadn't really *hit* me. Now it did. Like a Mack truck.

I couldn't see Mike and work on this screenplay. I didn't have the constitution to sleep with more than one guy. And I sure as hell didn't have the constitution to blow off Timothy and his "Baby, you've got it" spiel.

I had to break it off. Firmly. Cleanly.

I closed my eyes, feeling a little nauseous, then said what I had to say. "I, um, I don't think I can do dinner." I paused, knowing I should tell him the truth, then said, "I'm completely swamped at work."

Okay. So much for my attempt at utter truthfulness.

"Swamped," he said.

"Right. It's insane here. John's back from Rio, and we've got a dozen deals popping and—"

"That's okay. I understand. No worries."

"Oh." I wanted to exhale in relief, but I actually wasn't all that relieved. I wanted him to argue. To convince me. But all he said was, "Maybe we can find time next weekend."

It was only Sunday! That was days away! I wanted to howl in protest, but knew I couldn't. More, I knew I shouldn't. I needed to keep my eye on the prize.

And that meant Cullen.

I drew in a breath. "Sure," I said. "This weekend. Maybe we can squeeze something in."

The silence at the other end of the line was deafening. And long.

"Mattie," he finally said, his voice low and a little sad. "What's—" He stopped. "Never mind. This weekend then."

"Mike, I—"

"I need to run. Someone's at the door. Bye."

Then he was gone, and I was sitting there feeling like

an ass. And a determined ass, at that. Because if I just shoved away this guy who obviously liked me—and could make me come with little more than a look, and who made me laugh like no one else—then I was damn well going to make that shove worthwhile. I was getting Cullen. And I was going to nail the deal with Timothy.

And that was a subject not open to negotiation.

Determined, I hit the button for the speakerphone, then dialed Cullen's number, stabbing the buttons with the eraser of my red pencil. The phone rang once, twice, three times. I glanced at the clock. Already past eight. He was probably at dinner, about to start the party circuit.

Sure enough, the answering machine kicked on, and I heard his smooth voice announcing that he was out "having a good time," but if I left a message, we could maybe have a good time together. I resisted the urge to roll my eyes, and managed to leave a message without snickering.

I was just giving him my phone number for easy reference when I heard a click, followed by Cullen's voice. "Yo, Mattie, I'm here."

"Hey," I said brightly. Then I stopped. Then I started again, because I was on a mission. I closed my eyes, pictured an Emmy Award, and dove in. "Listen, I'm sorry we got separated last night."

"Yeah, well, you looked like you were having a good time."

"Oh, I was."

"With Mike, I mean."

"Oh. Right. Well, yeah, I was. But that doesn't mean—"

"Hey, I'm cool with that. We'd gone out for drinks. We had drinks. And then you wanted a little bit more than drinks. I can relate."

My head was swimming a little, and I wasn't entirely sure *I* could relate. But I pressed on. "Right. Um. The thing is, I was kind of hoping you and I could try again. I mean, we did the drink portion of the evening, but we never quite managed the date portion." *There.* I'd said it.

"Hey, that's cool," Cullen said. "Tonight?"

Actually, that night sounded good, and I knew I wanted to get the process moving. At the same time, I hadn't been joking when I'd told Mike I had a ton of work this week. And I really wasn't psyched up for tonight. "Friday," I said firmly. "I'm up to my ears in work until then."

"Friday," he repeated thoughtfully. "Busy night…"

"I know," I said. "I wish we could get together earlier, but I work for a production company, and we're in the process of rolling out a few new television shows. It's just so busy here right now." Okay, *that* was a blatant attempt at manipulation. But I'd picked up the copy of *Entertainment Weekly* that Timothy had mentioned, and from what I could tell based on the captions, Cullen The Model was gunning to be Cullen The Leading Man.

Suddenly, Cullen didn't think Friday night was all that busy after all. And, since my ploy worked, I didn't feel too guilty about the lie.

We agreed to meet at his place at seven, and then decide where to eat. "Get back to making good television," he said, his tone warm and involved. Honestly, if I didn't know any better, I'd think he was the kind who'd sleep with me just to get a television gig. I guess I had more in common with my male model neighbor than I'd thought…

I was considering that disturbing realization when my computer dinged, announcing the arrival of new mail. Since I never got much business e-mail on Sunday, I assumed the message was spam. An advertisement for Viagra or a link to porn or some such nonsense.

I shifted my mouse, causing the screen saver to melt away, and saw the message in front of me. Yup, definitely porn.

Are you wearing panties under your skirt? Are they damp?

Take them off, and slip your hand between your legs. All little girls working late deserve a break…and when you slip your finger inside yourself, you can pretend it's me—touching you—until I make you come.

Oh. My.

I shifted a little, frustrated by my reaction, and embarrassed enough by it that my hand moved automatically for the mouse, shifting the cursor over to the little icon that would delete the message.

I stopped just in time, my eyes focusing in on the sender of the message. I didn't recognize the e-mail address, but the name attached to the account was unmistakable: Mike Peterson.

I DIDN'T DELETE MIKE'S E-MAIL. For days, I stared at it, watching the cursor flash, reading the words, tallying up my slut points, and, yes, closing my door and doing just what it instructed.

What I didn't do was answer it.

I wanted to. So help me, I wanted to. I felt a pull to Mike like I'd never felt before. But pulling equally hard in the opposite direction was my entire life. My mom. My ambition. And my one shining opportunity.

How could I risk that?

I couldn't. I knew I couldn't.

And yet at the same time, a tiny voice in my head posed a single question: Would sleeping with Mike really risk it? Or are you just so mortified by what you're willing to do to get ahead that you can't bear to look him in the eye?

I tell you, sometimes self-awareness isn't all it's cracked up to be.

And, no, I wasn't mortified. I was a consenting adult. If I wanted to have a good time with Cullen and write about it for television, well, then, so what? I just needed to nip this thing with Mike in the bud. *That* was the problem. I'd let it hang over me for too long, like some unfulfilled promise. Or, more specifically, like the Sword of Damocles.

Once I cut it down, I'd be able to go on about the business of getting my life in order. More, I'd finally be able to shut the intrusive thoughts of Mike and his miraculous fingers out of my head.

Bolstered by my sudden revelation, I clicked on the e-mail and typed a reply:

No touching. No imagining. Just me working. It was fabulous and fun, but this has to be the end. Please, no more e-mails.

Not what I would call scintillating prose, but hopefully it would do the trick. It sounded understanding, but also slightly irritated. And, I thought, it didn't sound turned-on at all. Which, frankly, was a bit of a miracle considering that my panties were soaked through simply by the act of reading once through his message. *Touching you...*

For one second, I let myself wish that he could. And then I forced myself to press Send.

And that, as they say, was that.

10

FOUR DAYS. From Sunday night to Thursday night, Mike had absolutely no response to his naughty little e-mail. For that matter, he hadn't even seen Mattie, though he'd been looking.

He knew he was sunk, that his efforts to regain that connection with Mattie had failed. She hadn't said a word to him, but that silence spoke volumes.

She'd walked away, and he couldn't help but wonder if he'd pushed too far.

He was staring at his computer screen, debating the value of standing in front of her door and singing sappy love songs, when her e-mail arrived. He read it once, then a second time. It was short, businesslike, and to the point. She wanted him out of her hair. No more temptation. No more teasing.

No more sex.

He twined his fingers together and leaned back in his chair. *Interesting.* And—if he read between the lines—encouraging. Because Mattie wasn't telling him to get lost, she was begging him not to tempt her. To not try and prove to her that he was worth the temptation. That *they* were worth it.

Which meant that if he wanted to win this battle, tempting Mattie was exactly what he needed to do.

I HAD THREE BUSINESS CALLS after I sent the e-mail to Mike, which kept me at the office until well after ten, putting out various fires and chasing down various documents that just *had* to be located before shooting started in the morning.

For once, I didn't mind the late night, even though everything I was asked to do should have been addressed days before. After all, my headless chicken impersonation kept me running around the office. And that kept me not thinking about Mike. And that was a good thing.

Plus, the later I arrived home, the less likely that I would bump into Mike. So I was more than happy to pull into the parking area around eleven, then pause quietly in front of the bank of mailboxes before heading up to my apartment.

I had my mail in my hand and was flipping through a plethora of catalogs (yay!) and bills (ugh!) when I heard my name. I froze, the sound of that voice playing with my emotions in a way that both terrified and aroused me. And, frankly, pissed me off. I mean, hadn't I told him to leave me alone?

And yet there he was, walking toward me, his bare chest glistening in the moonlight, and a towel slung casually around his hips. I knew he was wearing a swim suit under there, but I couldn't see it, and my imagination conjured up a significantly less-clothed picture.

I swallowed, and tried to find my righteous indignation. "Mike," I said. "I'm surprised to see you."

"You are?" Surprise laced his voice, and I frowned. Hadn't he gotten my e-mail.

"Um, well, yes. I sent you an e-mail this afternoon."

"I know." He took a step closer. "I read it."

"Oh. Well." I tried to organize my thoughts. I can't say I was doing a heck of a job. "But then—"

"You said no more e-mails." His finger grazed the soft skin just below my ear, tracing a heated path down my collarbone, to the V-neck of my blouse, and down to my cleavage.

I tried not to, but I'm pretty sure I whimpered. And as much as I knew I should say something, I didn't. I couldn't.

That was okay, though, because Mike still had things to say. "You said no more e-mails," he whispered. "Trust me. What I have in mind doesn't involve cyberspace at all."

My heart stuttered in my chest. "Oh. I. Oh." I swallowed, wondering what had happened to my cold determination. For that matter, what happened to my resolve to focus solely and utterly on my career. Apparently it decided to go on vacation the second Mike came into view. I knew it would, of course. That's why I'd been avoiding the man.

I squared my shoulders, determined to be strong even if my willpower was fading. "Mike, I really need to get home."

"No."

"Pardon me?"

"Not yet. I have something I want to show you first."

"To show me?"

He held up a hand in a Boy Scout swear. "Honest."

"What?"

"If I could tell you, I wouldn't have to show you."

I crossed my arms over my chest and stayed silent.

"Come on, Mattie. Don't you trust me?"

"Yes, and no," I said.

He laughed. "Good answer." And then he took a step toward the stairs, looking back once to see if I was following.

I was.

What can I say? I was curious.

We headed up, then veered to the right toward his apartment. He opened the door and we stepped in. "Okay, what?" I asked.

"Turn around."

I shot him a questioning glance, but complied. To tell the truth, I was intrigued. I shouldn't have been. But I was. This was Mike, after all. And no matter how often or how loudly I told myself that I couldn't—shouldn't—care, I did. I really did.

So I turned around. And when he asked me to close my eyes, I did that, too.

The soft brush of his thumb grazed my cheek, and I swallowed a moan. This was *not* going anywhere; I couldn't let it. Wasn't he the man who'd said that the only reason I should ever feel ashamed of the path I'd taken in my life was if I chose not to follow an exit that led to what I wanted. I had that now. A clear path and a clear plan. I wished I could walk with Mike down the path, but I couldn't. I'd seen the path, I'd made my choice. And Cullen was the only man I had room for in my bed at the moment.

A nice little mental pep talk, to be sure, but it was hard to remember why I was so adamant about it when Mike slipped something soft and silky over my eyes. I tensed, but he bent low, his lips grazing my ear and his breath sending shivers racing through my body. "Shh." Not even a word, but that simple sound calmed me, and as my heart raced, he tightened the silk into a knot behind my head, effectively blindfolding me.

"Mike, we—I—"

This time, he silenced me with a finger to my lips. "I know you've been avoiding me. I know you want me to stop. I won't make you tell me why. All I ask is that you let me give you this night. No promises, no expectations. Just you and me and whatever happens inside this apartment."

"What happens in Mike's apartment stays in Mike's apartment?" I quipped, suggesting the popular Las Vegas slogan. I wasn't deliberately trying to make light, but I'd lost my boundaries. There, blindfolded, with his touch the only thing grounding me and his voice the only thing caressing me, I swear I wanted nothing more than to rip off my clothes and beg him to screw me.

So, naturally, I resorted to bad jokes.

And, since Mike knows me well, he ignored my ill attempt at humor. Instead, he moved straight into danger territory. He took my hand and led me farther into the apartment.

"Mike…"

"If you want to leave, say so now. Otherwise, don't say anything at all."

I opened my mouth, then shut it. Mike stayed completely silent, but I was certain I could hear him smile.

We walked just a few feet until he settled me in a straight-back chair. There was nothing erotic about sitting in a hard wooden chair, but I was so turned-on I was practically panting. Everything—his touch, his scent, the dark—conspired against me to make me wet, hot and very frustrated.

He knew; I was certain. For that matter, I was certain he intended to make me a lot more frustrated before the night was out.

Behind the blindfold, I closed my eyes. Then I sighed.

I really couldn't wait.

MIKE WANTED NOTHING MORE than to simply stand there and stare at the woman in his kitchen. The woman who, only hours ago, had sent him an e-mail basically telling him to stay out of her life. Now she was right here, blindfolded and vulnerable, for him.

He felt a surge of power mixed with tenderness. A heady combination, and as it surged through him he knew that, in fact, there *was* something he wanted more than to stand looking at her. He wanted to touch her. To make love to her. To lose himself in her.

And, most of all, he wanted to hear her scream his name.

Patience. What was it his Grandma Jo had said about patience? Good things come to those who wait?

He crossed to the freezer, trying not to grin. Well, that little saying was very apropos. Because he intended to make Mattie wait. And in the end, he definitely intended her to come.

"Mike?"

"Shh. I told you. No talking or I deliver you back to your apartment. Unless that's what you want?"

He held his breath, dreading the choice he'd just given her, especially when he saw her open her mouth. Then she closed it deliberately and gave one quick shake of her head.

His heart welled, and he tried to stay calm. Tried not to claim victory yet. Soon, maybe. But not yet.

He'd planned out a seduction, and now it was time to put it in play. Starting with the ice cube in his hand. The cube he held until the heat of his palm made it drippy and wet.

He brushed it over her lips, watching the way her tongue darted out for the coolness. Then he trailed it down her throat, leaving a glistening path that he lapped with his own tongue. Her breasts he teased with the cube, its frozen state causing her nipples to peak even under the professional blouse she'd worn to the office.

Without a word, he ripped the blouse off, sending buttons flying. She gasped, but didn't protest, and he felt himself harden, knowing that she was as into the moment as he was.

Lower and lower the cube went, until he was teasing her belly button, the muscles of her abdomen constricting with delight and passion. The cube was getting smaller, but he didn't speed up. Just went to work removing her skirt, leaving her clad only in panties and high-heeled shoes.

He bent down, as if worshipping at her feet, and then he took the ice cube and slowly worked it up her leg, paying special attention to the secret spots. Her ankle, the soft area behind her knee.

He took his time, wanting to make sure that she understood that he was doing this for her. That he wanted her. And that he intended to fight dirty to keep her.

He worked slowly for another reason, too. He wanted to prolong the pleasure. Soon enough, he'd lose himself inside Mattie Brown. But until then, he intended to lose himself in glorious, cock-stiffening, blood-burning anticipation.

I'D NEVER MADE LOVE BLINDFOLDED before, so I wasn't sure how I was supposed to feel. Nervous? Edgy? Exposed?

I guess I felt all of those things, but mostly I just felt turned-on. I didn't care how Mike touched me or if I could see him doing it. I just wanted the feel of him. The scent and sound of him.

And oh, dear Lord, the things he was doing to my body!

He dragged an ice cube up the inside of my leg, and I thrashed a bit, surprised by the contact. He held me down, gently, then tied my ankles with a silken scarf. And, yes, maybe that was a little much. Maybe that was even more cause for nerves. But I trusted Mike. I trusted what he was doing. And damned if I didn't get even more turned-on than before.

I wanted to beg for him to touch me. Slip a finger inside me. His cock. His tongue. But I kept silent, secure that this man would treat my body right.

He didn't disappoint me.

The ice cube melted its way to my sex, and when he brushed it against my clit, followed closely by the press of his thumb to counteract the cold, I screamed. And then I about passed out when he slipped the ice cube inside me, his tongue lapping up the liquid until I came.

He teased me more after that, making me come

again and again until I was sore and spent and utterly frustrated. I wanted him inside me. Wanted to beg for it, but not willing to do that.

He fed me strawberries, whispered my name, then licked the juice off my lips while his finger toyed with my clit bringing me, yet again, closer and closer.

This time, I couldn't stand it anymore. "Mike." I could only manage his name, and even that, only barely.

"I thought you'd never ask," he whispered.

I felt him untie the bonds on my legs, then help me to stand. I expected him to take the blindfold off or at least lead me to the bedroom. But he did neither. Instead, he pulled me back down again, and I realized that he'd seated himself, naked, on the chair. He spread my legs, grabbed my hips, and thrust me down hard, impaling me on him.

I cried out in both need and satisfaction, and as he held on to my hips, I rocked against him, tears streaming down my face and making the blindfold wet and mushy. I ripped it off, then looked him in the eyes. There was an intensity there, along with a promise.

And all of a sudden, I knew what had been lurking in my mind all along—this was the man for me. I'd been hiding from that fact, but it wasn't something I could escape. He was the one for me, and I couldn't compromise that by sleeping with some male model—even a nice one—simply to get a job.

"I love you, Mattie," he whispered.

I nodded, still crying. "I know. I'm sorry. I love you, too."

There it was. The God's honest truth. It felt good to say. Freeing.

But there was one thing I needed to do before I'd be truly free to love him.

MIKE LIVED ON THOSE THREE little woods all night and all day, which was easy, actually, since they made love three more times, and she said them at least that many more times.

Now, he was watching her get dressed, himself enjoying the luxury of spending Saturday in flannel pajama bottoms and the warm glow of sex. She'd told him that she had an appointment, and he was doing his damnedest not to grab her and shake her and ask her what exactly her plans for the evening were.

He hated the thought that she'd actually sleep with Cullen—even flirt with Cullen—simply to get a television gig. But he wasn't supposed to know about that, and saying something now would get Angie in trouble with her sister. More than that, though, he knew he had to let Mattie make her own decisions, however much he might hate them.

His resolve faded, however, after she kissed him goodbye. She left his living room, crossed to her apartment, then blew him a kiss. At first, he thought that was that. But then he saw her come out again, and this time, she didn't look in his direction. Instead, she went down the main stairs toward the parking garage.

He breathed a sigh of relief. The office. She was going to her office.

He was still standing by the window when he saw her come back. This time from the back stairway, the one near the laundry room. She walked purposefully to Cullen's apartment, knocked once, and waited.

And although he'd already decided to do nothing to stop Mattie, Mike couldn't stop the way his blood boiled as he watched Cullen open his door and usher her inside.

"MATTIE," CULLEN SAID, nodding a little as I stepped inside his apartment. "You look good."

"Thanks," I said. I'd left the door open a little. A psychological escape. Now I looked back at it and took a deep breath. "Um, listen, Cullen, about our date. I—"

"I can't do the date thing, Mattie," he said, which totally threw me off balance because that was my line.

"Huh?"

"I thought I could. Sleep with you, I mean. Because, I figured it would be totally worth it."

"Oh. Thanks. I'm flattered." I furrowed my brow. "I think."

"I don't mean because of you," he said, and then he grinned. That sexy grin that had driven me and Carla wild. "Sorry, that didn't come out right. I'm sure you're great. But I was thinking about the television show. It could be a break for me."

I took a step backward, eyeing him warily. Because how did he know about the show? I started to ask him, but he kept on talking.

"It's just not worth it," he said. "Not now that I've got someone in my life I actually care about."

I cocked my head. He really was repeating back to me everything I'd come here to say. "Who—" I began to ask, but he spoke over my question.

"I hope you don't mind. I know you were counting on the show."

I felt myself smiling broadly, and I reached out to grab his hand. "I don't mind at all," I said. "In fact, I came here to cancel our date. I'm…well, I'm in love with someone."

"Yeah? Mike Peterson, huh?"

I nodded, feeling light as a cloud.

"Good for you." He pulled me close, hooking an arm around me in a brotherly sort of hug.

Brotherly...

That's when everything fell into place. How he knew about the television show. Why he'd been spending so much time with Angie. And who he "actually cared about." Cullen, it seemed, was in love (or, at least, in lust) with my sister. Who, it just so happened, emerged from the bedroom looking rumpled and satisfied.

I swallowed a squeak of surprise and a squeal of horror as anger ripped through me. I wanted to lash out at her. To ask what the hell she was up to. But I couldn't get the words out because I couldn't quite believe that my sister would stoop so low. She'd led Cullen along. Seduced him, even. She'd told him about the show and edged herself into the mix. All in a transparent attempt to win some nonexistent competition with me about who would get Cullen!

And Cullen didn't know. I could tell from his face that he'd really and truly fallen for my sister.

Dear Lord. What had I started?

I pulled him into a hug, wishing I could tell him the truth, but knowing now wasn't the time. Instead, I just gave him a squeeze, and hoped that the touch felt genuine and happy instead of sad and regretful.

I was still holding him when the door slammed open and Mike barged inside.

"Dammit, Mattie, I thought I could handle it, but I can't."

Cullen and I jumped apart, and Angie trotted down the stairs to join us. Mike, it seemed, hadn't noticed Angie. He was looking only at me.

"Don't do it," he said. "I don't have any right to ask you to make choices about your career, but I have to ask anyway. I have to ask because I love you and I can't bear the thought of you sleeping with someone else."

His words hung in the room, at first delighting me, and then causing a slow burn of fury to burn through me. I turned, looking in the direction of Angie and Cullen, and saw Mike turn that way, too. For the first time, a hint of confusion crossed his face. "What—"

"I'm not going to sleep with Cullen," I said. "I came here to tell him that. Interestingly, he already knew about the television show, too."

I looked pointedly at Angie, who quickly diverted her eyes.

"When did she tell you?" I demanded, stepping close and poking Mike in the chest. "For that matter, *what* exactly did she tell you?"

"I told him everything," Angie said in a small

voice. "Not too long after you two…you know…the first time. Movie night."

I didn't look at her. I kept my eyes on Mike. "So all this time, you *knew?* About the slut test and the television show and all of it?"

"Mattie, I'm—"

I shut him up with a slap across the face, then leaped back, startled by my own fury. But I had reason to be furious. With him and with Angie. With Mike, though, the pain was even deeper. I'd come to believe in something real, only to find out he was simply part of my sister's master plan to win Cullen for herself. Words flew from my tongue before I could even think about them, all the hurts and fears just pouring out of me. "Was everything between us an act? Some perverted attempt to up my score? Satisfy that part of poor little Mattie's angst? Make things so interesting that I forgot about Cullen? Damn you!" I was beyond reason, but I felt betrayed. By both Mike and by Angie.

I needed air, and I brushed past Mike to get it. He started to follow, but I turned and flashed him a look of cold steel. He stopped. And I went on to my apartment.

And when I got inside, I threw myself on the bed, and I cried.

MIKE SENT MATTIE A DOZEN ROSES every six hours for the next five days, seeking redemption. He'd failed her, and he knew it. Not only had he not trusted her, but he'd toyed with her, just as she'd accused him of doing, even if not for the purpose he'd accused her of.

That horrible day in Cullen's apartment, he'd wanted to deny it. To tell her that she was wrong. That every time they'd made love someplace other than a bed, he hadn't thought to himself, *Yes, for this I have scored a point.*

The truth was, he *hadn't* thought that way. At least not that brashly and deliberately. Their time together had been sacred to him, and his only thoughts had been for her pleasure, and of his own.

But he couldn't deny that his knowledge of her slut test score, along with her resolution in the laundry room and her ultimate plan to seduce Cullen, had colored his perceptions. That and the knowledge that a major cause of her doomed relationship with Dex had been partly due to complacency in bed. Mike didn't want to be complacent. And so he made himself go out of his way to be daring and exciting. Made himself think that making love in the bathroom of a dance club was a good idea. Made himself send an erotic e-mail.

He'd done those things because he knew she craved a sensual excitement; that she felt as if that had been missing from her life. And the truth was, he didn't regret one single thing.

The only thing he regretted was that he'd learned about her longing without her consent. She felt violated and used. He understood that; he really did. And he hated himself for being the one to make her feel that way.

Worse, he didn't know what he could do to make amends. And he *had* to make amends. Because the one thing that Mike had learned throughout all of this was that he couldn't survive without Mattie in his life.

I DIDN'T WANT TO WEAKEN, but I was anyway. How could I not? My apartment had more flowers than a florist, and if Mike sent any more, I'd have to move to a hotel just to have room to walk about.

"He's totally in love with you," Carla said, pushing aside a vase of yellow roses, the latest to arrive via delivery, right on schedule. "Don't you think you've made him suffer enough?"

That got my blood boiling again. "I'm making him suffer? What about what he did to me? What he and Angie both did to me?"

"What about it?" she said. "I mean, yes, maybe Angie started out in competition mode, but she didn't stay there. And now she's head over heels in love."

I closed my eyes, hiding my frustration. Carla was right. I knew she was right. And yet I still wasn't quite ready to see him. "He used my secrets against me," I whispered. "I don't know how to get past that."

"It's not like he read your diary," Carla said. "And yes, Angie shouldn't have told him about you going after Cullen or about the television show, but the girl was falling in love herself."

I grimaced, but reluctantly nodded. Cullen wasn't what I'd pictured as my sister's type, but it had turned out that they'd totally hit it off. Angie had explained everything. About how she'd started hanging around him because of the competition between us. But then something had shifted and it had begun to feel real. They'd started seeing each other, and she'd told him about the television show, hoping that he'd laugh and tell her no way would he go on a wild sexual exploration with me simply to get a shot at a pilot. Cullen, however, hadn't said that at all. He wanted the television show, and was willing to do just about anything to get it. I couldn't fault the guy. I mean, I'd been doing the same thing.

And so they'd had a fight and Angie had stormed out. I'd overheard the whole thing, and hadn't even realized.

After that, Angie had spilled her guts to Mike, both wanting a shoulder to cry on and help. The rest, as they say, is history.

"And to tell you the truth," Carla said, "I think what he did was kind of sweet. I mean, if Mitch got wind that I thought my sex life was dull, and then he secretly tried to ramp it up... Well, how cool would that be?"

I shot her a disbelieving look, and she shrugged. "Not that my sex life *is* dull, but you know."

I wanted to deny it and say that I *didn't* know. But I did. I really did.

Even more, I knew this wasn't really about the sex. My hesitation was about me. I felt like a first-rate ass, and I was a little baffled that Mike would even still want me. After all, in an effort to advance my career, I'd completely discounted my life.

When I told Carla as much, she just shrugged, then waved her arm, encompassing the umpty-zillion vases of roses. "Somehow, I don't think he's holding it against you. And besides, he's the one you need to be talking to. Not me."

I drew in a breath, then closed my eyes, imagining Mike in front of me. Being in Mike's arms again. Feeling Mike's kisses.

Was I willing to throw all that away because he'd

gone out of his way to spice up my sex life? Put that way, the notion was ridiculous.

I needed him, and I believed he needed me.

Most of all, though, I needed him to understand that I'd finally discovered what was really important in life. All these years, my mom had it wrong. Career is fine, but it's love that counts.

I'd found love with Mike. And I damn sure wasn't going to lose it now.

I KNEW MIKE WANTED TO make up. I mean, that was obvious from the flowers. The many, many, many flowers. But even so, as I stood in front of his door my stomach twisted and flipped, nerves getting the best of me.

I gathered my courage, lifted my hand and knocked.

At first, he didn't answer, and I wondered if he wasn't home. Or, worse, if he'd looked out his peephole, seen me, and realized that I wasn't the woman he wanted after all.

But then I heard the lock click. The knob turned, the door swung open, and there he was, the smile on his face telling me that everything was going to be all right.

"Mattie," he said, his voice full of love and longing. He reached for me, but I took a step back, determined to say what I had to say.

His eyes narrowed, wary and hurt, and I rushed to reassure him. "I love you," I blurted, erasing the worry on his face with those three simple words, and lifting my heart in the process. "But I have to say something first."

"So long as you're not telling me to get out of your life," he said, "you can say anything that you want."

"I don't want out of your life. Not now. Not ever." My eyes welled, and a tear trickled down my cheek. "But I have to apologize."

"You don't owe me an apology."

"I do," I said. "I let my career get in the way of my life. I was taking risks to further my career, but it never occurred to me to take a risk to further a relationship. I almost missed out on love because I was too stupid to follow it."

"But you did follow it," he said with a smile. "You're here, aren't you?"

I smiled back, feeling warm and happy and relieved and loved. "Yeah," I said. "I am." And this time, when he reached for my hand, I took it.

"HAPPY?" HE ASKED. We were in my bed, and he pulled me close, his warm eyes sweeping over me, loving and possessive.

"Oh, yeah." I nodded, then pressed my face

against his chest and breathed deep, my heart rejoicing. I'd taken a risk, and it had paid off. In winning Mike, I'd won everything I'd ever wanted. Everything, that is, except…

"What is it?" he said. "What's wrong?" He pulled back a little, then hooked a finger under my chin and tilted my head up to face him.

I made a face, but shifted so that I could sit up. "It's really nothing," I said. "Just my competitive nature on overdrive."

"How so?"

I considered for half a second, then launched into it. "Don't take this the wrong way, but I'm now right back where I started from. Not on the slut test," I amended, flashing him a wicked grin. "I think it's a fair guess that you and I have managed to build that score up to a very respectable level. And not on my life path." I gave him a squeeze. "There, I'm exactly where I want to be."

"You're thinking about your career."

"Guilty," I said.

"I'm listening."

I lifted a shoulder, then let it drop. "I had the chance to write the pilot episode of a television show right in my hand," I said. Then I reached over and stroked his chest. "Now I have you, and I'm not complaining, but—"

"Why can't you have both?"

I blinked. "What do you mean?"

"Have you told Timothy you're not going to turn anything in?"

"No, not yet." I'd been too chicken to bring that up. "Carla may have said something, though."

"I doubt that," he said. "I think Carla figures you can handle your own career."

"Because my track record is so good…"

"Everyone has to start somewhere," he said. "Why don't you start with your slut score?"

"But that's the point," I said. "That's exactly what we pitched to Timothy. But the story hinged on increasing the score with Cullen. You're just not—"

"A ratings draw? Yeah, I know. That keeps me up at night." I hit him with a pillow, but he kept on. "Aren't you forgetting that Cullen's still a part of your story? A big part, actually. You just never slept with him. A little oversight about which I'm extremely grateful."

"And now that he's dating Angie…." I sat up

straighter as the ideas started to spin. Then I kissed him. Hard. "Mike, you're a genius."

"I know," he said with a wry grin.

"And you're about to be immortalized on the screen. Oh, man, this is…" I trailed off, tossing the blanket aside as I got up, naked, and headed toward the living room and my desk.

"Hey, it's 3:00 a.m. Where are you going?"

"Fall in love with a writer," I tossed back, "and this is what you're going to have to put up with."

I heard him sigh, then heard the rustle of sheets followed by his footsteps. I was booting up my laptop when he came and pressed a kiss to the top of my head.

"You don't have to stay up with me," I said. "Get some rest."

"I fully intend to," he said. "But first, I'm going to make you a pot of coffee."

I smiled to myself, warmed by his words. *Making me coffee.* If that wasn't true love, I didn't know what was.

I tilted my head back and smiled, then accepted the kiss that he offered. Then I shooed him away. "No reading over the shoulder."

He laughed, and moved back to the kitchen. I settled in to type.

FADE IN.
INT. LAUNDRY ROOM—DAY
Mattie
Eighteen percent! Eighteen percent is for nuns and small children!

* * * * *

*Experience the anticipation, the thrill of the chase
and the sheer rush of falling in love!
Turn the page for a sneak preview of a new book
from Harlequin Romance
THE REBEL PRINCE
by Raye Morgan.
On sale August 29
wherever books are sold.*

"OH, NO!"

The reaction slipped out before Emma Valentine could stop it, for there stood the very man she most wanted to avoid seeing again.

He didn't look any happier to see her.

"Well, come on, get on board," he said gruffly. "I won't bite." One eyebrow rose. "Though I might nibble a little," he added, mostly to amuse himself.

But she wasn't paying any attention to what he was saying. She was staring at him, taking in the royal blue uniform he was wearing, with gold braid and glistening badges decorating the sleeves, epaulettes and an upright collar. Ribbons and medals covered the breast of the short, fitted jacket. A gold-encrusted sabre hung at his side. And suddenly it was clear to her who this man really was.

She gulped wordlessly. Reaching out, he took her

elbow and pulled her aboard. The doors slid closed. And finally she found her tongue.

"You…you're the prince."

He nodded, barely glancing at her. "Yes. Of course."

She raised a hand and covered her mouth for a moment. "I should have known."

"Of course you should have. I don't know why you didn't." He punched the ground-floor button to get the elevator moving again, then turned to look down at her. "A relatively bright five-year-old child would have tumbled to the truth right away."

Her shock faded as her indignation at his tone asserted itself. He might be the prince, but he was still just as annoying as he had been earlier that day.

"A relatively bright five-year-old child without a bump on the head from a badly thrown water polo ball, maybe," she said defensively. She wasn't feeling woozy any longer and she wasn't about to let him bully her, no matter how royal he was. "I was unconscious half the time."

"And just clueless the other half, I guess," he said, looking bemused.

The arrogance of the man was really galling.

"I suppose you think your 'royalness' is so obvious it sort of shimmers around you for all to see?" she challenged. "Or better yet, oozes from your pores like…like sweat on a hot day?"

"Something like that," he acknowledged calmly. "Most people tumble to it pretty quickly. In fact, it's hard to hide even when I want to avoid dealing with it."

"Poor baby," she said, still resenting his manner. "I guess that works better with injured people who are half asleep." Looking at him, she felt a strange emotion she couldn't identify. It was as though she wanted to prove something to him, but she wasn't sure what. "And anyway, you know you did your best to fool me," she added.

His brows knit together as though he really didn't know what she was talking about. "I didn't do a thing."

"You told me your name was Monty."

"It is." He shrugged. "I have a lot of names. Some of them are too rude to be spoken to my face, I'm sure." He glanced at her sideways, his hand on the hilt of his sabre. "Perhaps you're contemplating one of those right now."

You bet I am.

That was what she would like to say. But it suddenly occurred to her that she was supposed to be working for this man. If she wanted to keep the job of coronation chef, maybe she'd better keep her opinions to herself. So she clamped her mouth shut, took a deep breath and looked away, trying hard to calm down.

The elevator ground to a halt and the doors slid open laboriously. She moved to step forward, hoping to make her escape, but his hand shot out again and caught her elbow.

"Wait a minute. *You're* a woman," he said, as though that thought had just presented itself to him.

"That's a rare ability for insight you have there, Your Highness," she snapped before she could stop herself. And then she winced. She was going to have to do better than that if she was going to keep this relationship on an even keel.

But he was ignoring her dig. Nodding, he stared at her with a speculative gleam in his golden eyes. "I've been looking for a woman, but you'll do."

She blanched, stiffening. "I'll do for what?"

He made a head gesture in a direction she knew was opposite of where she was going and his grip tightened on her elbow.

"Come with me," he said abruptly, making it an order.

She dug in her heels, thinking fast. She didn't much like orders. "Wait! I can't. I have to get to the kitchen."

"Not yet. I need you."

"You what?" Her breathless gasp of surprise was soft, but she knew he'd heard it.

"I need you," he said firmly. "Oh, don't look so shocked. I'm not planning to throw you into the hay and have my way with you. I need you for something a bit more mundane than that."

She felt color rushing into her cheeks and she silently begged it to stop. Here she was, formless and stodgy in her chef's whites. No makeup, no stiletto heels. Hardly the picture of the femmes fatales he was undoubtedly used to. The likelihood that he would have any carnal interest in her was remote at best. To have him think she was hysterically defending her virtue was humiliating.

"Well, what if I don't want to go with you?" she said in hopes of deflecting his attention from her blush.

"Too bad."

"What?"

Amusement sparkled in his eyes. He was certainly enjoying this. And that only made her more determined to resist him.

"I'm the prince, remember? And we're in the castle. My orders take precedence. It's that old pesky divine rights thing."

Her jaw jutted out. Despite her embarrassment, she couldn't let that pass.

"Over my free will? Never!"

Exasperation filled his face.

"Hey, call out the historians. Someone will write a book about you and your courageous principles." His eyes glittered sardonically. "But in the meantime, Emma Valentine, you're coming with me."

SAVE UP TO $30! SIGN UP TODAY!

The complete guide to your favorite
Harlequin®, Silhouette® and Love Inspired® books.

✓ Newsletter ABSOLUTELY FREE! No purchase necessary.

✓ Valuable coupons for future purchases of Harlequin,
Silhouette and Love Inspired books in every issue!

✓ Special excerpts & previews in each issue. Learn about all
the hottest titles before they arrive in stores.

✓ No hassle—mailed directly to your door!

✓ Comes complete with a handy shopping checklist
so you won't miss out on any titles.

SIGN ME UP TO RECEIVE INSIDE ROMANCE
ABSOLUTELY FREE
(Please print clearly)

Name

Address

City/Town   State/Province   Zip/Postal Code

(098 KKM EJL9)

Please mail this form to:
In the U.S.A.: Inside Romance, P.O. Box 9057, Buffalo, NY 14269-9057
In Canada: Inside Romance, P.O. Box 622, Fort Erie, ON L2A 5X3
OR visit http://www.eHarlequin.com/insideromance

IRNBPA06R   ® and ™ are trademarks owned and used by the trademark owner and/or its licensee.

Introducing an exciting appearance
by legendary
New York Times bestselling author

DIANA PALMER

HEARTBREAKER

He's the ultimate bachelor...
but he may have just met
the one woman to change his ways!

Join the drama in the story of a confirmed
bachelor, an amnesiac beauty and their
unexpected passionate romance.

"Diana Palmer is a mesmerizing storyteller
who captures the essence of what
a romance should be."—*Affaire de Coeur*

Heartbreaker *is available from Silhouette Desire*
in September 2006.

Visit Silhouette Books at www.eHarlequin.com   SDDPIBC

HARLEQUIN *Blaze*

"Super-
steamy!"
—*Cosmopolitan*
magazine

New York Times bestselling author

Elizabeth Bevarly

delivers another sexy adventure!

As a former vice cop, small-town police chief
Sam Maguire knows when things don't add up.
And there's definitely something suspicious happen-
ing behind the scenes at Rosie Bliss's flower shop.
Rumor has it she's not selling just flowers.
But once he gets close and gets his hands on her,
uh, goods, he's in big trouble…of the sensual kind!

Pick up your copy of

MY ONLY VICE

by Elizabeth Bevarly

*Available this September,
wherever series romances are sold.*

www.eHarlequin.com   HBEB0906

If you enjoyed what you just read,
then we've got an offer you can't resist!

Take 2 bestselling love stories FREE!

Plus get a FREE surprise gift!

Clip this page and mail it to Harlequin Reader Service®

IN U.S.A.	**IN CANADA**
3010 Walden Ave.	P.O. Box 609
P.O. Box 1867	Fort Erie, Ontario
Buffalo, N.Y. 14240-1867	L2A 5X3

YES! Please send me 2 free Harlequin® Blaze™ novels and my free surprise gift. After receiving them, if I don't wish to receive anymore, I can return the shipping statement marked cancel. If I don't cancel, I will receive 6 brand-new novels each month, before they're available in stores! In the U.S.A., bill me at the bargain price of $3.99 plus 25¢ shipping and handling per book and applicable sales tax, if any*. In Canada, bill me at the bargain price of $4.47 plus 25¢ shipping and handling per book and applicable taxes**. That's the complete price and a savings of at least 10% off the cover prices—what a great deal! I understand that accepting the 2 free books and gift places me under no obligation ever to buy any books. I can always return a shipment and cancel at any time. Even if I never buy another book from Harlequin, the 2 free books and gift are mine to keep forever.

151 HDN D7ZZ
351 HDN D72D

Name	(PLEASE PRINT)	
Address	Apt.#	
City	State/Prov.	Zip/Postal Code

Not valid to current Harlequin® Blaze™ subscribers.

Want to try two free books from another series?
Call 1-800-873-8635 or visit www.morefreebooks.com.

* Terms and prices subject to change without notice. Sales tax applicable in N.Y.
** Canadian residents will be charged applicable provincial taxes and GST.
   All orders subject to approval. Offer limited to one per household.
® and ™ are registered trademarks owned and used by the trademark owner and/or its licensee.

BLZ05   ©2005 Harlequin Enterprises Limited.

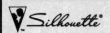

INTIMATE MOMENTS™

Don't miss the next exciting romantic-suspense
novel from *USA TODAY* bestselling author

**Risking his life was part of the job.
Risking his heart was another matter...**

Detective Sawyer Boone had better things to do
with his time than babysit the fiercely independent
daughter of the chief of detectives. But when
Janelle's world came crashing around her, Sawyer
found himself wanting to protect her heart, as well.

CAVANAUGH WATCH

Silhouette Intimate Moments #1431

When the law and passion
collide, this family learns
the ultimate truth—that
love takes no prisoners!

*Available September 2006
at your favorite retail outlet.*

Visit Silhouette Books at www.eHarlequin.com   SIMCW

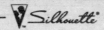

SPECIAL EDITION™

COMING IN SEPTEMBER FROM
USA TODAY **BESTSELLING AUTHOR**

SUSAN MALLERY

THE LADIES' MAN

Rachel Harper wondered how she'd tell
Carter Brockett the news—their spontaneous
night of passion had left her pregnant!
What would he think of the naive
schoolteacher who'd lost control? After
all, the man had a legion of exes who'd
been unable to snare a commitment, and
here she had a forever-binding one!

Then she remembered.
He'd lost control, too....

**Sometimes the unexpected
is the best news of all...**

Visit Silhouette Books at www.eHarlequin.com   SSETLM

Blaze

Sue Johanson's Hot Tips

Forbidden Fantasy #4

Knowing your lover's secret desires/fantasies

If you want to take your sex life to an exciting new realm, consider these tips for sparking the imagination:

The Write Stuff

Create a "fantasy grab bag" with your partner by each writing down various scenarios you would love to act out in the bedroom. Don't reveal your personal wish lists in advance. That way, when you select a slip of paper from the grab bag, one of you will always be surprised!

~or~

Movie Night

Rent a DVD that represents a genre you might have fun reenacting, be it a romantic costume drama or an edgy cop thriller. Once you and your sweetheart have finished your viewing party, the two of you can have fun thinking up your own sexy sequel!

Sue Johanson is a registered nurse, sex educator, author and host of The Oxygen Network's Talk Sex with Sue Johanson.

Photo courtesy of Oxygen Media, Inc.

HARLEQUIN®

Blaze™

COMING NEXT MONTH

#273 MY ONLY VICE Elizabeth Bevarly

Rosie Bliss has a little thing for the police chief. Okay, it's more than a *little* thing. But when she propositions the guy, she gets a mixed message. His hands say yes, while his mouth says no. Lucky for her, she's a little hard of hearing….

#274 FEAR OF FALLING Cindi Myers
It Was a Dark And Sexy Night... Bk. 1

As erotic artist John Sartain's business manager, Natalie Brighton has no intention of falling for him…even though something about him fascinates her. But when mysterious things start happening to her, she has to wonder if that fascination is worth her life…

#275 INDULGE Nancy Warren
For a Good Time, Call... Bk. 2

What happens when you eat dessert…before dinner? Mercedes and J. D.'s relationship is only about sex—hot and plenty of it. Suddenly the conservative lawyer wants to change the rules and start over with a *date!* What gives?

#276 JUST TRUST ME... Jacquie D'Alessandro
Adrenaline Rush, Bk. 2

Kayla Watson used to like traveling on business. But that was before her boss insisted she spy on scientist Brett Thorne on his trek into the Andes mountains. Now she's tired, dirty…and seriously in lust with sexy Brett. Lucky for her, he's lusting after her, too. But will it last when he finds out why she's there?

#277 THE SPECIALIST Rhonda Nelson
Men Out of Uniform, Bk. 2

All's fair in love and war. That's Emma Langsford's motto. So when she's given the assignment of recovering a priceless military antique, nothing's going to stop her. And if sexy Brian Payne, aka The Specialist, gets in her way, she has ways of distracting him….

#278 ANYTHING FOR YOU Sarah Mayberry
It's All About Attitude

Delaney Michaels has loved Sam Kirk forever…but the man is too dense to notice! She wants more from life than this, so she's breaking free of Sam to start over. But just as she's making a clean getaway, he counters with a seductive suggestion she can't refuse!

www.eHarlequin.com

HBCNM0806